Guide

Also by Dennis Cooper

Try

Frisk

Closer

Wrong

Jerk (with Nayland Blake)

Horror Hospital Unplugged (with Keith Mayerson)

The Dream Police: Selected Poems 1969–1993

Guide Dennis Cooper

Grove Press
New York

The epigraph is taken from *Arthur Rimbaud: Complete Works*, translated by Paul Schmidt (Harper & Row, 1975).

Thanks: Ira Silverberg, Colin Dickerman, Carla Lalli, Morgan Entrekin, Elisabeth Mitchell, Amy Gerstler, Vincent Fecteau, Terminator, Linda Roberts, Ann Cooper.

Published simultaneously in Canada
Printed in the United States of America
FIRST EDITION

Library of Congress Cataloging-in-Publication Data
Cooper, Dennis, 1953–
    Guide / Dennis Cooper. — 1st ed.
       p.   cm.
    ISBN 0-8021-1608-6
    I. Title.
    PS3553.0582G85   1997
    813'.54—dc21   96-49020

DESIGN BY LAURA HAMMOND HOUGH

Grove Press
841 Broadway
New York, NY 10003

10 9 8 7 6 5 4 3 2 1

For Joel Westendorf

"So what if a piece of wood discovers it's a violin."
—Arthur Rimbaud

Contents

Guided by Voices   3

The Freed Weed   25

Sunshine Superman   45

Blur   67

Star-Shaped   97

The *Spin* Article   127

Epistle to Dippy   153

Guide

Guided by Voices

Luke's at Scott's. Mason's home jerking off to a picture of Smear's bassist, Alex. Alex's jeans are so tight you can make out his ass. It's sort of nondescript, like a kid's. Robert, Tracy, and Chris are several miles across town shooting dope. They're so fucked up. Pam's directing a porn film. Goof is the star. He's twelve and a half. I'm home playing records and writing a novel about the aforementioned people, especially Luke. This is it.

"Robert. You screening calls?" Luke listened. "Guess not." He hung up.

"They're still not *home?*" asked Scott's mosquitoey voice. It tended to tremble, squeak, wheeze half-inaudibly.

"Depends on what you mean by 'home.'" Luke smiled mesmerizingly, he could just tell. Then he let his thought patterns crap out to the music.

Guided by Voices: Everything fades from sight / because that's all right with me.

Luke's sweet, deep, a little paranoid, and perpetually on. Just twenty-five, he has chocolatey shoulder-length hair, a thin face, big, wild eyes, and a tall, narrow body disguised by loose clothes. Scott, thirty-two, is an artist who shows with a hip local gallery. Balding and schlumpy, with an agreeable, unshaven face, he's overeducated, spaced out, and extremely neurotic.

"Luke, you're too metaphysical for words." Scott smiled . . . sarcastically?

"Whatever." Sometimes Scott totally weirded Luke out. Luke grabbed for the phone. "I'll call Mason."

Scott stood up and clomped in the bathroom's direction.

"Mason," Luke said when a nasal voice answered. "We're out the door."

Then Luke sits for a half minute, eyes glazed, absorbing Guided by Voices. Their fractured, archaic pop stylings are not to his taste. He's into trippy, computer-built, danceable soundscapes. So he has a little daydream re Chris, this acquaintance of mine, Robert's, Tracy's, and Mason's. Chris is a disturbed twenty-two-year-old junkie/porn star who looks like an elongated child. In reality, they've never spoken. In Luke's fantasy, they're at the used CD store where Chris works, and their eyes accidentally meet. There's a flash of recognition. It could be emotional, spiritual, sexual, whatever. The details don't matter.

Scott reentered the living room, sat.

"Déjà vu," Luke muttered. He'd seen Scott reenter the room in that exact way before. Time was he'd have figured such thoughts were just fallout from LSD, DMT, Ecstasy. . . . Now he knew they were magical.

Guided by Voices: Oh, I . . . / wouldn't dare to . . . / bring out this . . . / awful bliss.

"*Really?*" Scott asked with his usual amazement. "You saw me walk in here *before*? We-ei-ird."

†

Once I dropped acid three times a day for a month. It was the summer, my sixteenth. My family was taking our yearly vacation on Maui. I'd made this friend, Craig, a local surfer with great drug connections. Every morning we'd score a few blotter hits, hitch-hike to this remote beach, and spend the day zonked, hallucinating, babbling, and swimming around in the ocean. After several weeks, we started to lose it. We'd found this coral reef a short distance offshore. One day we robbed a hotel room, stole a truck, and transported the room's furnishings to the beach. We towed our loot, piece by piece, through the surf, underwater, and into this huge, cavelike nook in the reef, setting each chair, rug, et cetera, in place, then swimming furiously back for the surface. Our plan was to live in this cave, rent-free, far away from fascistic reality. It never crossed our minds that we wouldn't be able to breathe.

Mason was waiting in front of his building. Tallish and slim, he had a newborn goatee, tiny eyes, and an ironic manner. Seeing Luke's car, he gave a tidy little wave that was a bit self-parodic.

"Hey," the trio announced in a cluster.

As they drove, Mason declaimed about the beauty of Smear's bassist, who'd just inspired a new group of his famous collages.

One afternoon we were hitchhiking out to our favorite beach when a carload of young Hawaiian natives pulled up. They half-jokingly ordered us into their car. Being fried, we agreed. It was a known fact that most of the locals hated white tourists, whom they accused of gentrifying their island. They especially hated the hippies. And with our long hair and cutoffs, we qualified. As they drove, the car's occupants taunted us. One whipped out a knife. I don't remember too well, but somewhere along the way they announced they were going to kill us. Craig played along. But I started crying and pleading with them, which I guess spoiled their fun, since they pulled the car over and ordered us out. They drove off. We were safe, but I couldn't shake off my hysteria. For the next maybe ten or so hours I lay by the side of the road, convulsing, screaming, flailing my arms and legs uncontrollably, hallucinating so hard it was like being constantly punched in the face, while poor Craig tried in various ways to attract me back into the real.

"Is this funereal enough?" Tracy fed the new Guided by Voices CD into the player and punched track 15. "There." She rose to her feet.

Out poured a charred, thudding song redolent of the early punk era but sweetened, perhaps in production. Within seconds an irony-drenched vocal sliced through, and Tracy returned to the couch, eyeing Robert suspiciously.

"Kind of," said Robert. Like Tracy, he was short, pale, watery-featured, and twenty. His deep-set blue eyes were consistently sad, but his voice had a brittle, imperious manner, which made him unpopular, hence lonely. Hence that look in his eyes.

I've successfully blocked out those ten scary hours, but they were the worst and most profound of my life. I felt completely alone and lost. In my few clearer moments, between hallucinations, I believed I'd gone totally insane, or what people characterize as insane, and suspected I'd never return to the world, in which Craig, acting as the unofficial ambassador for everyone I'd ever known, saw me off with such bewildering tenderness. I wasn't confused. Despite my explosive behavior, I felt an unusual clarity. I knew more than I'd known, and yet, as part of my mental upgrading, I understood how this "genius" would isolate me. All that otherworldly information, so suddenly focused, available, et cetera, had no accompanying language. But in describing my state, I'm unable to note more than its skimpiest outline. That's my point. How can I bring what I learned in that world into my everyday consciousness, then translate those thoughts into palatable terms, even assuming the knowledge is still in my brain somewhere? It's one of my big goals in life.

"Kick him," said Robert. He pointed at Chris, whose long, slight, androgynous body lay spookily still on the carpet. It had a Pietà-esque twist.

In the background, Guided by Voices blared away, giving the situation a tense, darkly comical spin.

Tracy shrugged. "If he's dead, he's dead."

"Well, what if he's dying?" Robert's eyes attacked hers, although, mentally at least, he was horrified, period.

Chris had been drugging himself in death's general direction for years, to his friends' mild amusement. In a way, they were partly to blame, having offered half-jokey encouragement, supplying heroin, works . . . not to mention their numerous, lengthy discussions of suicide and so forth. Tonight he'd crossed the line, it appeared. His "minute to rest," i.e., his little struggle with bad nausea, had lasted . . . two unnervingly motionless hours, more or less.

Tracy dipped the pointy tip of her shoe into Chris's black jeans and gave a very slight push.

Guided by Voices: When you motor away / beyond the once-red lips . . .

"Oh, shit." Robert stuck out his shoe, kicked. Chris slid a half foot toward the door. His hands did little flip-flops. The palms bloomed. His face sort of . . . slackened, is one way to put it.

Guided by Voices: When you free yourself / from the chance of a lifetime . . .

Among recreational drugs, only heroin and LSD access the sublime, to my knowledge. Still, their styles are completely dichotomous. LSD can make anyone brilliant—temporarily, at least—but there's a catch, i.e., it also renders one freakish, inarticulate, an idiot savant uncomprehendingly jailed within the crude rights and wrongs of the world's "sane" majority. Opiates, on the other hand, tend to instigate a flirtation with death, which, of course, is a physical state one can only romanticize, which, as a consequence, makes one's flirtation with dying inherently profound, since "profound" and "unknowable" are synonyms, right? But serious opiate use can lead to actual death, and while dying lets users transcend their society's simplistic presumptions, it leaves the dead person's life and beliefs vulnerable to the lame revisioning of the long-lived.

In the Whisky's dim men's room, Luke and Scott stood in parallel stalls, shaking piss off their dicks.

"LSD," said a weary voice.

Luke zipped up, did a three-quarter turn.

"It's Owsley," continued a tall, sunburned, skateboardy kid with blond dreadlocks. His eyes radiated a cut-rate malevolence. "Made to the specifications of the old hippie chemist himself," he continued. "So it's fierce shit."

One more thing while I'm remembering it. A year, maybe two, before my Mauian flip-out—when I was fourteen, I think—I did mushrooms with five or so friends. One of them, Lee, a half-Korean pianist, began to hallucinate so furiously that he exited his body—or so it appeared, since his face lost all warmth and tore wide open, every orifice flared in a grotesque silent scream. The sight totally unsettled the rest of us. Well, all except for his girl-friend, who wasn't stoned, and who kept studying his wrenched, frozen face, then turning to us and whispering, with a huge, clueless smile, "God, I want to be *in* there with him." That moment has really stayed with me, I don't know why.

"Wh-wha . . . ?" Chris mumbled. He raised his head.

"Chris," Robert said, trying to sound unperturbed. "We should go. If we want to catch Smear at the Whisky, I mean."

Tracy was hunched over, cooking a shot for the road. The spoon blackened, crusted up, et cetera, in the tip of a skinny flame.

They each do a shot. Then they sprawl around for a few minutes, nodding out, nodding in. Robert organizes them into a unit that fits through the door, down the street, and into Tracy's truck, which he insists upon driving, being a total control freak. En route, each one thinks spacily about death. To Robert, death is the enemy. When it's a subject, he broods, period. Tracy weighs dying's positives and negatives. To her, death means suicide, an act she contemplates almost every day as a way to . . . control her life? Chris just wants to die. It's been his lifelong obsession. To become dead as gradually and with as much intricacy as is humanly pos-sible. He wants to feel himself fading away from one world, fading into what's next. There'd be a point, he imagines, when he would be simultaneously dead and alive. For that moment, however tiny, he'd know everything there is to know about human existence.

I'm playing an LP that came out the summer I took too much acid. As soon as the needle eased down on its crackly surface, that experience flashed back.

The phone rings. Shit. "Hello, yeah," I say into it.

"It's me." Luke was barely a rip in some distorted pop music. Smear's "We're So High," by the sound of it.

"Luke," I blurt. "Hey." I just totally fucking adore Luke.

"Listen, you won't believe this," Luke yelled. "Scott and I just dropped acid. But nothing's happening yet."

Chris works at a used CD store. For kicks he collects children's literature and acts in cheap porn films. He's relatively asexual, but not from confusion. Sex just isn't an issue, except when he needs some quick cash or wants badly enough to be friends with someone who's attracted to him. He blames drugs, which have helped him evolve. He's been stoned in one way or another since he was eleven. Drugs' pharmaceutical kick has circumvented whatever makes sex so supposedly sublime. Chris doesn't need people, at least not in that lovey-dovey, spiritual way. All of which gives him a slightly ethereal air. So he's kind of invisible—to most peers, at least. But every once in a while, a certain woman or man will obsess on him. Mostly abject, artsy types, for some reason. Being passive and drugged out, he's easily drawn into others' emotional gravity.

When Chris, Robert, and Tracy lurched into the Whisky, Luke hugged them, especially Chris.

Smear: We're so high / We want to fall all over you.

Robert nodded out, in for the band's entire set. Smear seemed fine, no big deal. He supposed they were cute. When the house lights came up, he asked Mason, who was both gay and intelligent, "What did you think?"

"That I want to have sex with the bassist."

I want to name-check the record I'm playing, since its dated style is influencing my words. It's Donovan's *Mellow Yellow*. Donovan was an acid-head folkie who put out two brilliant late-60s LPs, then kicked drugs, went New Age, and became the embarrassing space case his name brings to most people's minds. For a brief time he managed to translate the tone of an LSD high into exotic yet palatable songs. They're more souvenir-like than knowledgeable, but they do draw a sketch, however kitschy in tone, of that particular mental locale. Beneath their lame "period" surface, I can detect an eerie hint of enlightenment's siren.

Sunset Boulevard curved to the left . . . right . . . left . . . right . . . Its shapeliness made Robert want to get high, but what didn't?

"Can you drop me at Pam's?" Chris asked. He'd been slouched in between his friends, lost in forgettable daydreams. I starred in one, for a second.

"Sure." They'd stopped at a light. Robert and Tracy were trading fierce, miserable winces encoded with tons of interpersonal bullshit.

For years after my ten-hour freak-out, I wouldn't touch drugs. Then they filtered back into my lifestyle again, one by one. Except for acid, the mere idea of which gave me a mild nervous breakdown. Still, memory's weird. And there came this one night when . . . But I'm getting ahead of myself. Point is, some of the drugs I was using—pot, hashish, speed, mushrooms, Ecstasy—referenced my acid trip, but in a manageable way, sort of like documentary films do their nonfictional subjects. I would experience a shadowy form of the original freak-out, and the proximity thrilled me. So I started to flirt with my long-lost insanity, with drugs' assistance. Some nights I would wind up so mentally gone that my drug-buddy friends had to slap me around, trying to coerce me back.

†

As Luke drove, the freeway lost . . . something.

What if the stars are the sky, and the sky is the stars? Scott was thinking. He studied the windshield. If the blackness is solid, a wall, and the white bits are speckles of light that have escaped from whatever's just past that black barrier.

In the backseat, Mason sat, eyes unfocused, imagining collages.

That's where the truth is, Scott thought. In that whiteness the sky keeps away from our knowledge. What if a 747 were flown into one of those specks? Wouldn't . . . that . . . ?

A year ago, when I was writing for *Spin* magazine, the editor asked me to spend a few days with an HIV-positive, homeless teenager named David and his gang of friends, then write up what happened. One of David's friends was a tall, blond, angelic punk rocker and part-time street hustler named Sniffles. He asked me to buy him, and maybe because I was lonely and sort of depressed at the time, I did. Thing is, he liked to be hit and slapped around, and even though my imagination's a freezer compartment for violent thoughts, I'm a wuss. I was into crystal meth at the time, and before we went to bed I chain-snorted a gram. Crystal makes me psychotically horny. Sniffles had just dropped some Ecstasy, so he was feeling all warm and invulnerable. Anyway, things went a little insane. I intend to go into the details, just not at the moment. First, I need to arrange a few things so I'll feel more at ease.

As soon as I open the front door, it's obvious. "Shit, you guys are really fucked up," I say, looking from Luke's stricken face to Scott's, Mason's.

"Not me," Mason said. And he wandered inside.

Scott veered past my shoulder. "Oh, *boy*," he said, blinking. "Where's the . . . living room?"

Scrounging around in one pocket, Luke found, produced the last hit of acid. "Throw this away," he insisted. "Immédiately."

It's spooky how Ecstasy floods one with indiscriminate affection. It's a chemical lie. It kills thought, undermines sensibility. LSD, on the other hand, neatly demystifies sex. It can. I remember. On a great acid trip, you begin to realize the insidious way lust distorts almost every decision we make. Acid encourages us to embrace isolation, to disempower other human beings, especially their bodies. When LSD works, it makes clear how inane and addictive sex is, and how culture's overvaluation of physical contact keeps us from a true understanding of life-and-death issues. Maybe this lesson has particularly struck home in my case, since my fantasy life is so sexual in nature and murderous in content.

"Later, guys." Chris, hugging himself to keep warm, trotted into a typical, faintly lit mini-mall. When he turned to wave bye, his friends' truck was a dot.

On the truck's staticky radio, Pavement's "Cut Your Hair" cross-faded into . . . uh, Guided by Voices?

"Let's fucking end it," said Robert. The idea arrived out of nowhere. Words just . . . formed, disconnected from everything else. He thought for a second, then steered toward some oncoming traffic.

Tracy's eyes watered. "Okay," she said. And she covered her face.

I'll say this once. I'm extremely fucked up. It doesn't show, but I am. Over the years I've developed a sociable, generous side, which I train on the people I know. It makes them feel grateful, which

makes me feel purposeful. But secretly, I'm so confused about everyone and everything. Sometimes these moods will just come out of
nowhere and lay me out. I'll curl up in bed for long periods of time,
catatonic and near-suicidal. Or I'll space into a murderous sexual
fantasy wherein some cute young acquaintance or stranger is dismembered in intricate detail, simply because he's too painfully
delicious, i.e., through no fault of his own. But LSD cured this
psychosis—in hindsight, at least. That's why I'm going to slip, as
"recovery" types like to say. Because for ten long-lost, jumbled-up
hours I'd known a kind of . . . whatever, peace? That's my current
belief.

       "Luke's so . . . amazing," I say, knowing that word's limita-
tions. I'm thinking about . . . well, pretty much everything about
him. "It's just overwhelming, you know?"
       "You think?" Mason asked. "I guess I can vaguely remember
deciding so once."
       Something about the black shirt Scott was wearing made
Luke sort of astral-project into . . .
       "Where's that kiddie porn tape?" Mason asked. He'd crouched
down by the shelves where I keep CDs, videos.

This is sort of a secret, but Chris and I are involved. The whats,
hows, wheres, whys will come along later. Suffice it to say that
Chris is my type. Then factor in his death wish, which is neatly
aligned with my aforementioned dreams. Problem is, now that my
fantasy's so doable, I can tell how complex the thing is. I'm not
just stupidly tranced by the prospect of killing some boy during
sex, even if that great idea's been a bit too ignited by Chris's and
my interactions. Anyway, I'm sort of torn between Chris, who
accesses the evil in me, and Luke, whom I'm beginning to love in
a pure, unerotic, devotional way that I never would have thought

myself capable of even four months ago. And I have to make a choice, or I want to. Actually, I've made my choice. That's why Chris has to go, I don't know how.

A twelve-year-old kid stands around in Pam's studio, giggling. Marijuana smoke honks in and out of his freckled little nose. He has a delicate build and extremely black hair.

Chris shoots him a look of, well . . . sadness, bewilderment, jealousy. Some combination of those.

"Want a toke?" the kid asks. A shaky hand holds out the joint. "'Cause . . ." His eyes get confused. ". . . uh . . ." His jaw drops an unflattering inch, his eyes glaze. The whole face kind of . . . stiffens, as if it were made out of clay and Pam's place were a kiln.

Scott saw through Luke. Literally. The guy was a multihued mist. Luke, staring back, noticed something elaborately off-key in the world. Because Scott's eyes were too . . . dried out. When Luke wasn't there, beyond stoned, in a friend's living room, appreciating the fibrous texture of . . . what's-his-name's eyes, his view was blocked, thoughts mechanically consumed by a weird hallucination, i.e., he kept driving his car over a squashed, sizzling dog on some intensely overlit desert road. Really, over and over and over.

"Amazing," I say, studying Luke's gone expression. "How long . . . ?"

A purplish-red orb strobed intently somewhere in Luke's universe.

"Don't ask me," Mason said from my kitchen. He cracked the fridge. I heard a beer bottle gasp. "First they kept saying how fucked up they were. Then they shut up completely. So . . . since they shut up, I guess. Twenty minutes?"

I'm studying the pill. "Want to split this?"

†

I've tried to reconstruct my acid-fueled nervous breakdown on Maui, because between brief bouts of horrified consciousness, wherein my difference from everyone else in the world seemed profound, I saw such intense things. Have I said that already? But the experience is lost—or polluted, at least—by a bevy of earlier trips, and some later "flip-outs"—say, my insane sex with Sniffles, or my entanglement with Chris. The memories are weirdly inseparable, blurred, I don't know why. Maybe there's something to getting incredibly stoned, then having sex with self-destructive young guys, that resembles the world acid showed me. But there are differences, too, which I hope to define.

Robert was maybe just maybe one-quarter alive but . . . Tracy was definitely dead. No fucking doubt a-fucking-bout it. Because she was . . . upside down?

Guided by Voices: The hole I dig is bottomless / But nothing else can set me free.

Tracy couldn't . . . quite . . . think, but she could sort of, um, sense a kind of . . . haze, hiss. "Um . . ."

Robert moved his head very, very slightly. Oh, excellent.

The skin on Luke's face was a fog. Scott could see, or almost see, his friend's skull or, more specifically, that curious object which certain historical types once so lazily labeled "the skull." It was more like a pkhw . . . Words failed Scott. A filament? But weren't words too complex to manipulate properly? Luke, for instance, meant nothing compared to the word "Luke," because it defined a million people named Luke. Or take "love." "Love" was the world's favorite word. But it was also a lie that human beings made up to avoid actual knowledge, which was itself a lie. Or "cancer." "Cancer" was a word that encapsulated a thought which had never reached clarity, which was why the disease was incurable. If Scott could think clearly from morning till night every day of his life, he would never get cancer. Oh, my God. It was so fucking simple. No, it was.

"So what's going on, Pam?" Chris lets out some smoke. "Here, take this." He hands the joint back to the kid, who pinches, looks down at it.

"Nothing." Pam's gazing daydreamily at what's-his-little-name, who's very slowly tamping out what's still around of the joint in a nearby ashtray.

"So," Chris says, turning to the kid. "What's your name?"

"Huh?" The kid blinks himself away from some thought asteroid. "What?"

Goof, a.k.a. Nicholas Klein, is a horridly parented twelve-year-old. Before he got sucked into drugs, his whole life was nightmarish. Now he's okay, sort of. Good sense of humor. Hence his nickname. Still, one shouldn't let oneself get too attached, because he's dying. Right now, unbeknown to him, thanks to some undiagnosable problem in one of his heart valves or something. But it'll work out okay. No one will miss him, and thanks to a brief stint costarring in kiddie porn videos, he'll leave behind a vital body of work that'll only be more resonant with the knowledge he's dead. Trust me.

Robert was haze—on the inside, at least. Thoughts sort of . . . frittered around. Skinwise, forget it. Might as well go ahead and die than . . . live . . . like . . .

Tracy: xklijmpprtizk . . .

Robert just bought it. Internal injuries. He . . . hazed. Emptied out. Refilled with something too complicated for words.
Robert: knxggsvzkqtt . . .

Pam's not so bad. If she could express how she feels, she'd be
motherly, even. Apart from her thing for young boys, she's a dyke
with an ongoing serious relationship. Physically, she's large, a
former fat girl turned comfortably husky, not without a shitload
of effort. Her hair's brownish and short, her clothes casual, bland,
and male-esque. Like me, she's fascinated by kiddie porn. Unlike
me, she can justify making the stuff for a living. Until recently
I could justify watching it, period. Now I'm confused. As a way
to help Chris overcome his obsessive death wish, I've instigated
a project, a kind of pseudo-snuff kiddie porn film to be scripted
by me, starring Chris, and directed by Pam. I'm thinking it
might be a safe, effective way for Chris and me to semi–act
out our intermeshed fantasies once and for all, not to mention
make Pam infamous on the kiddie porn circuit, which I believe
is her goal.

Mason studied Scott's awestruck or horrified face. "What do
you think they're . . . seeing?"
I swallow the pill. "Hard to know," I say, handing Mason his
beer. "Luke, Scott? Can you hear me? Hey!"
Luke's eyes are greenish . . . no, hazel . . . no, aquamarine,
with a spray of brown speckles and kind of, uh, yellowy smears.
Scott heard not words but a million or so little tones that
were so beautifully interlinked that he got the idea to record someone saying those words, then release it on CD.

Luke's eyes are the immediate clue to his greatness. Without them,
he'd just be a sweet-looking raver—on first glance, at least. They're

large, multicolored, and often glazed over in serious thought. That's
a guess. Anyway, they seem complicatedly wired. It's awe-inspiring
to be in his presence. Especially that night, thanks to acid. Luke,
meanwhile, was smiling unseeing at my awestruck face, having checked into another reality. He could tell that what he'd en-
visioned was wrong on a technical level. Still, he believed it was
real. At the same time, he could think lucidly on his ridiculous
state, i.e., Why would my mind construct this? How exactly does
LSD work? Then the clarity would erode and he'd be watching a
purplish-red orb flash rapidly on a depthless black field, thinking,
Wow.

"I'm Goof," says the kid. He holds out one hand.

Chris gives it a shake. "Great name." Then he glances at Pam,
who looks much less . . . well, distant than usual. "What're you
thinking?"

"Just . . ." Pam says, ". . . about the project with Dennis.
Wondering if Goof could play you as a kid."

"Sure, why not?" Chris says, wondering how to change the
subject to heroin. He gives Goof a cursory peer. "Maybe . . . if you
dyed his . . ." A yawn eats the sentence.

Chris would rather not crash there at Pam's, but what with sleepi-
ness being so fascistic, it's not like he has any choice. So he asks
her if he can take a very short nap, half an hour at most. "Sure,"
Pam says, and kindly finds him some dope and a clean set of works.
Then Chris mock-salutes Goof, who's too out of it or whatever to
notice, and scuffs into a little room just off the studio where Pam
shoots her porns, kicks the door shut, and whips off his way stinky
T-shirt, jeans, Nikes. Cooking his shot, he thinks and simultaneously tries not to think about me. But his hazed imagination
keeps ensnaring my face in its web or whatever.

†

"This works fast," I say, turning to Mason. "If I space too far out, stick around, keep an eye on me, yeah?" And even as I say this, I'm spacing out.

"Will do," Mason said. He was over by my VCR, crouched, doing something.

Donovan: Looking through crystal spectacles / I can see I had your fun.

Scott was . . . outside, yeah. In a . . . driveway?

Scott was standing in somebody's driveway. Oh, yeah, Luke's. There was Luke, perched on the hood of a car. He was talking, gesturing, et cetera, but Scott couldn't hear shit. No, that's not true. He heard whooshing. Actually, the sound was extremely refined. Someone had obviously composed it. No, wait, Luke's mouth was emitting it. Shit. Trying to sort out the details, Scott leaned back on a hedge. But the surface of leaves was flimsier than it looked, and he plunged into the depths of the plant's slightly springy brown skeleton, then had to claw his way out.

"Hold on," Pam says. "Before you go, I think I owe you some money."

"Cool, thanks." Goof digs around in a pocket. "'Cause I don't know if I'll see you again." He slides out a comb. "I'm going to . . . change my life."

Pam's counting out twenties. "Really?" She extends about seven, eight. "Well, then, am I entitled to one last request?" And she eyeballs his crotch.

"God, you're gross," Goof yells, half-joking. "All right, all right. But . . . I get to pick out the sound track." And he runs toward a Guided by Voices CD.

†

I met Chris through Robert and Tracy. Occasionally I'd shop at the store where he worked. Since he was my type, I'd developed a harmless, persistent little crush like one does. I forget how the subject came up, but I told them that I was attracted to Chris, and they told me how Chris had been known to trade sexual favors for dope. One night I dropped by the store around closing time, dropped a few hints, offered to buy him heroin, and we spent an extremely strange night at his place. Sexually, he was open to anything safe, but he didn't give a shit the whole time very obviously. Let's just say he was pliable. And with all that freedom, and fueled by his self-destructive urges, I guess I went sort of insane. I intend to go into the details, just not yet.

Scott stared into something beyond the constraints of human language.

Luke's eyes are so mesmerizing they're practically . . . what? I study their swirly, multiplicitous color for what seems like days, thinking, Wow.

Donovan: Dow dow dow dow . . . dow dow . . . dow . . . dow dow.

Luke stared into something beyond the constraints of human language.

"Mason," I say. He's playing a video. Kiddie porn, I think. "I'm . . . going."

I'm practically gone. Luke and Scott are gone. There's no point in describing their mental locales. Just accept that they're in two very vast, complicated, non-narrative states. Me, I'm still flashing in and out of what we call reality. Mason has put on a kiddie porn tape that Pam lent me, three hours of Super 8 films poorly transferred to video. Goof co. .ars in eight or nine of them, coincidentally. He's a favorite of mine. In fact, once when I accidentally blink the real world into place for a couple of seconds, Goof's ass is this splayed, perfect, shimmering, televised orb in my peripheral vision. Normally, seeing his ass in that state would fire off a violent daydream, but—thanks to the acid, I'm sure—it seems more like a . . . whatever, bric-a-brac. Kitsch. So when a finger appears on the screen and is shoved up the ass, I literally don't understand. In other words, I'm in a better place.

Mason spaced out, daydreaming. In his fantasy, Goof's slutty asshole belonged to Smear's bassist. And that finger was Mason's.
Luke, Scott: klvxmhspwwlqhx . . .
"God," I say. "This is . . . so . . . intense." I'm looking at something in Luke's staring eyes that you wouldn't understand.
Mason glanced over at us. All's well, he thought. Still . . . "You guys okay?" Nothing. So he reburrowed his eyes into Smear's bassist's "body."

Truth is dry. You'll know the truth when everything in your world seems as if it's been cooked until nothing is left but the exact information that separates it from other things in the world. On acid, you look at a thing, anything, with complete understanding. At the same time, everything's more mind-boggling than ever. And that combination's the truth. It's as if the brain power you normally waste fantasizing re sex, love, et cetera, had been redistributed to your nonhuman contacts, i.e., between you and a . . . I don't know, TV set or whatever. Something finite.

Pam's sculpting two teeny clown hats out of Goof's giant nipples. From the look on his face, he seems very, very into it.

Guided by Voices: I'm too tired to run from the tiger / I'm too dumb to hide in the bushes.

Suddenly there's this, like, unbelievable pain. Upper chest. "Oh, *fuck*." Goof gasps, gasps, gasps, balls his fists. *"Please . . . stop."*

The very second Pam frees up Goof's nipples, he dies. Empties out. Looks all weird. Crumples up on the floor.

And then there was one. I mean one rational mind in the story. I.e., mine. Everyone else was asleep, dead, in shock, drugged, or horny. Comparatively, at least, I maintained a kind of semi-sobriety, by virtue of Luke, who, out of it as we were, held my faltering interest, I don't know why. Love, weird. So, hoping to stay in that half-aware state, I pulled out the notebook and pen I always carry around and began to take notes on my surroundings, occasionally adding a cryptic bit of analysis. Not that anything brilliant showed up on the page.

The Freed Weed

It was minutes to closing. A loud, repetitive, dense guitar riff made the store feel unreal and sort of sinister. It could have been old Spacemen 3. Maybe "O.D. Catastrophe," weirdly enough. Chris was leaning on one of the cash registers. He had a pale, impish face, blond, disorganized hair, and a slim, lanky body that drove me insane. When our eyes met he shone, period, for a few seconds there.

"I'm . . . Dennis?" I took a vague step or two in his direction.

"Oh, right." He turned down the music.

"You're Chris. Robert's friend."

"Oh, right." He folded his arms and seemed to blink the store's depths into focus. "Actually, Robert hates me."

I guess I looked confused.

"Robert's trying to kick. So he's against knowing people like me because of . . . you know, his withdrawals and that. But fuck him."

"Yeah, fuck him." Now that Chris mentioned it, there was this junkie-esque weight to his voice. It sort of dragged through his words, like it couldn't be bothered with what he was thinking.

"So you're a junkie."

He gave me a quizzical squint, which he almost immediately wiped. "Off and on," he said. Then his face kind of . . . sturdied, in pride, I think. "I make porns." He sniffled. "Star in them. Or I used to."

"Really?" I'd been inching his way. "Any chance of seeing them?"

From the way his eyes changed, he'd picked up on my interest. They warmed, which sort of normalized his features. I mean, to me he was already perfect. But to most of my friends, he was only okay. I guess you either fetishize fucked-up young guys or you don't. Anyway, he brightened. Really, it was as if someone had just cleaned a century of grime off some masterpiece.

Chris was scanning the store's wildly postered decor. "Okay, what are you doing now?" And his eyes flashed at mine. They were definitely warm.

"Now's fine."

"Because I have this idea." He leaned very close. "Check this out." His breath smelled sweet but kind of ugly, like incense. "Give me some money for dope," he said, "and we can watch porn all night, if you want." He grinned sweetly. "I get really, really friendly when I'm high. Sometimes I shock myself."

"Deal." I fished out my wallet and emptied the contents. Three twenties. They flapped on the counter.

Chris snickered. "A man on a mission," he said. He picked up the bills and smashed them into one pocket.

I reached for his ass. I mean, all of a sudden, like I was grabbing the wheel of a runaway car. That's not my usual style, but I guess I was really caught up. Junkies are sort of unreal in a way. Every signal's so faint. You could hunt through their features forever and never see one fucking trace of your presence. So you might as well act all self-focused yourself. Because junkies respect other narcissists. Or that's my experience.

Chris laughed, muttered something I couldn't quite hear. "I'll go score," he added. "Meet me at my place in an hour."

"You live in the Fontenoy, right?" Chris's ass was so flimsy it seemed to deflate in my hands. I could feel the small, ornate archway of his hipbones. I might as well have been polishing them with a very soft rag.

Chris stiffened slightly and eased his lower body from the puzzle of my grip. "Yeah. Number eight," he said. I guess my caresses were too complicated or whatever. I've been told that before.

I shoved my hands into my pockets.

"The buzzer doesn't work." Chris backed toward the shelves where the store kept special orders, box sets, et cetera. He misjudged the distance and smacked into one of the rows with his ass, knocking things loose. A few CDs clacked to the floor.

"I understand."

"Uh . . . see you soon, then." He made a one-eighty turn and started straightening up.

I left the store and drove around for a while, killing time, dreaming up sex acts. Chris was flotsam, period, every enterable point on his body wide open. When I fantasize about sex, it tends to look like a fire, or like a big pack of shuffling cards, my desires are so furious. Inside that blur, which even I can't completely transgress, it's impossible to tell if I'm worshiping some guy or torturing him. Probably both.

†

"Hey!" I was squinting down a long, narrow, badly lit hallway with nothing on its walls. "You there?"

Chris materialized. He'd switched into a toddler-size T-shirt and loose jeans which rested so low on his pale, bony hips that an inch of pubes smoked from his belt buckle. "Yeah, hi," he said.

"How's it going?"

"Better." He shook my hand limply. "In the kitchen. Straight ahead."

Two seconds later, things lit up around us. Once upon a time, the room had been 50's-ish cool, with hysterically patterned wallpaper and dozens of knicknack shelves, now spiderwebby and littered with matchbooks. The furniture, counters, dirty dishes, were polka-dotted with roaches, apparently frozen in shock.

"Want a bit of the dope?"

The roaches sprayed into various cracks.

"No, thanks."

Chris opened the fridge, bent way over, and reached deep inside, moving bottles and beer cans around. The back of his T-shirt raised up, exposing a glary patch of skin, much of it ass. Most of my friends are into pumped, boxy asses. But I like them near-nonexistent. Junkies' asses are perfect, partly because they're so scrawny and, at the same time, being so constipated, such weird treasure chests.

I sat at the table and lit a cigarette, pulling a food-caked plate close as my ashtray. Desire was undoing me.

Chris sat down across from me, organizing his dope, works, spoon, bleach, lighter, cotton balls, into a rough semicircle. Cooking his shot, he'd glance up on occasion and smile, gritty-eyed, anticipating the heroin's rush, I guess.

"You know, I'm not that great in bed," he said, hunting a vein. "I'm easy, though. That's the best part. Hey." He found a spot, slid in the needle.

"Don't you tie your arm?" I asked.

"Old wives' tale." Then his eyes batted. "Whoa. Nice." He eased out the emptied syringe. Within seconds, his blank, sort of Swedishy features had morphed into a sunken-eyed, pointy-chinned gargoyle's.

"You all right?"

"Definitely," said his voice.

I spent about a half minute studying him. He looked like a corpse. Like he didn't belong to this world anymore. Calmer and much more together, I mean.

"What are you . . . experiencing?" I tried.

"Oh, it's nice," he mumbled. "Give me a second." He almost smiled, I think.

Chris's kitchen held very few clues about him. It looked sporadically used, and smelled very faintly of rotten food, period, which just meant the fucker was semi-disorganized—like all youngish guys, basically.

I heard a crash, squeak.

"Uh . . . we should do this." Chris had teetered away from his chair. He entered the hall, staggering, bumping into walls, hunched over like an elderly man.

"Hey, hold on a second."

When we got to the . . . living room, he headed straight for the TV, pushed POWER, and crashed to the floor, nodding out as a beautiful image defogged in its rectangle. "One . . . second," he whispered.

†

On TV, a slightly too beautiful child—male, I think—eyed the mouth of a cave. The volume was down, but I suspect there was a dangerous sound track. He stepped inside, cocked his head, cringed, then took another few steps. Suddenly there was a shift in perspectives. I was inside the cave, looking back at the child. He was edging my way. Then something human-esque rose up between us and blocked him out.

"Some of these go way back," Chris said. He fed the VCR. "So don't be shocked."

The TV screen held an antique-looking image, two small boys walking hand in hand down a crooked dirt road.

"Jesus, how old were you here?" I squinted through the multi-multi-copied tape's yellowy fog. The boy on the left was unquestionably Chris, albeit blonder, scaled down, and a bit cutesy-wootsy.

"Eleven." He landed midfloor, cross-legged, not far from the TV. "Can you see?" he asked, dragging himself a foot or so to the right.

In the video, Chris and friend stroll for a while. The road is muddy and lined on both sides by scruffy little pines. Chris wears black shorts, a tight yellow T-shirt, knee socks, and white Nikes. He has a rolled-up sleeping bag gripped in one hand. The other boy is wearing a huge purple T-shirt and baggy blue jeans. He's Hispanic, a foot or so taller than Chris, and, oh, twelve, thirteen?

"What's the other boy's story?" I asked, pointing.

"I'm not sure," Chris said. "Some kid. Nice enough and everything."

"Were you into him?"

"Oh, uh . . . I guess."

The Hispanic was cute, but he paled next to Chris, who was totally exquisite the way some kids are. "Well, you're obviously the star here."

"I was pretty cool, wasn't I?"

"Definitely."

"Yeah, thanks."

The children enter a clearing. Chris unrolls the sleeping bag. The Hispanic boy strips. He has a slim, athletic body, immense genitals, and a violent tan line. Chris is smoothing the bag, oblivious, when the other boy sneaks up behind him and yanks off his T-shirt. They collapse on the bag, kissing furiously, with Chris's pale, ribby back to the camera.

"Were you actually kissing?" I asked.

"Sure, man." Chris looked over his shoulder, studying me, eyes pinched in . . . confusion, I think. "People used to be into me."

"They still are," I said, fixing my eyes on the screen.

"Yeah?" said Chris's voice almost shyly.

I couldn't risk meeting his gaze for some reason. I sort of hate it when things get too obvious. "Yep." And I cleared my throat.

The children are nude. The Hispanic boy is sprawled on his back. Chris is up on all fours, straddling him in the opposite direction. He's kissing the head of that oversize dick. The Hispanic boy is yanking on Chris's. It's minuscule. Occasionally he raises up slightly and gives it a doggy lick. Whenever this happens, Chris tenses and throws back his head.

†

"Felt good?"

"What do you think?" Chris's shoulders just slumped. "It's all coming back." He shook his head.

I'd sprung another hard-on. It was cramped painfully within a fold of my jeans. So I unsnapped, unzipped them, and slid it out into the open. But that action made more noise than I had expected.

Chris turned, blinked. "You gonna put that in me?" he asked —jokily, I think. Then his eyes jetted sideways, rejoining the video.

"To say the least."

Chris's face gravitated toward the TV, whose ugly light blasted it. "So what are you into again?" he asked, blinking. "Not that I care."

"Asses," I said, stroking myself to make blatancy easier. "You know, sort of doing your ass in every possible way, if . . . you don't mind. I mean, safely, of course."

Chris shook his head. "Anything's okay if I'm fucked up enough."

The Hispanic boy holds Chris's ass crack wide open and grins at the camera. Off in the less-focused distance, Chris's bobbing head gives him a blow job. One of the Hispanic boy's fingertips tests the springiness of Chris's asshole, then sinks to the knuckle. The hand looks gigantic, Chris's ass sort of doll-size in contrast. When the finger withdraws, the hole unfurls.

I could sense my face flushing. "So . . . how did you . . . uh, how did this . . . feel?"

"It felt good," Chris said.

"How . . . experienced were you?" I was beginning to zone. In my daydream, Chris's adolescent ass was an inch from my face.

Chris's head turned again, really twisting his neck. His eyes were slits, like little brush strokes. "Why? Don't I look like I know what I'm doing?"

"Sure, no, that's not what I meant, but—"

On TV, things changed with a bright flash of hazed-over color. The children had shifted locales to a bedroom and were speedily undressing again.

"What's this . . . ?"

"A man's coming in," Chris said. "I think he's supposed to be what's-his-name's father. I never could figure that out."

The children lie on a double bed, kissing. The door opens a crack. A balding Hispanic man, maybe fifty, peers in, spots the children, and grins. He enters, walks straight to the bed, and separates them. The Hispanic boy skitters away. The man grabs Chris's arm, pins him down on the bed, and licks his ass for a while. At one point the man raises up, says a few words, and laughs.

"I'm sure you don't remember what he said."

"No, I do," Chris said. "He said . . . I remember this perfectly . . . he said, 'You're like cream in the shape of a boy.'" Then Chris quarter-turned, eyed me, arched an eyebrow, and cracked up. In so doing, his face just . . . flew open. Teeth, gums, tongue, completely visible. To be honest, it didn't do his features any favors.

"How'd you respond?"

"Oh . . . I thought it was nice, I think. Didn't I?" He quit laughing and scrunched up his face. That looked better. "Yeah, sure."

"You didn't think he was gross?"

"No, uh . . . I just wanted him to like me."

"Did the camera bug you?"

"Sometimes. Like this shit." He waved at the TV. "Being rimmed was fucked up."

"Were you turned on at all?"

"I don't think so."

"Hm." I squinted at Chris's fuzzy little face, and, yeah, it did look sort of pleased as opposed to transported.

"It's weird," Chris said, watching his younger self. "With heroin, I'm sort of back in that kid state again. Because you can't come. That's why hustling's okay. It just means that people like you." His eyes glazed a bit. "Do you have a boyfriend?" He turned, studying me, though it didn't appear that he could see very much.

"No." I really must have liked him to say that.

The Hispanic boy is sidelined, calmly smoking a joint. The man, who's in a wild sixty-nine pose with Chris, reaches over and finger-fucks him to be nice or whatever. The man's face is wedged between Chris's splayed legs, which are spasming a little. Chris is blowing the man as best he can given the vastness of the dick and the puniness of his mouth.

"This is intense," I said, stroking myself at a fast yet safe clip.

"Yeah," Chris mumbled. "I can see that. But I was starting to wish it was over. Because the man got too . . . something."

I squinted at the TV. Little Chris seemed "into it," period. "You can't tell," I said.

"I didn't want anyone to know."

The video cut to a new pose. Chris was lying flat on his back. The Hispanic boy had sat down on his face. The man finger-fucked Chris. Chris was holding one of his legs in the air, presumably so future viewers could see where the finger and asshole connected.

"I know this looks hot," Chris said. "I mean, it's exciting me, too." He twisted around, raised one knee, so I could see a dinky hard-on engraved in his jeans leg. "But I was really, really ready for it to be over."

Chris rims the Hispanic boy. His eyes are dilated and blinking. After what he'd just said, I could see he was miserable. Still, I'm almost sure that if I'd been watching the porn by myself, sans commentary, I would have been thinking, So this is how ten-year-olds register ecstasy. It's strange how ambiguous everything is, especially children, who just seem like gods when you don't have to deal with them personally.

"Did they pay you?" I asked, trying to sound more concerned than I was. Honestly, I just felt delirious and anxious to fuck him.

"Yeah," he said. "And they gave me some pot."

"So . . . I was thinking that . . . maybe we could . . . sort of . . . go ahead?"

Chris glanced back at me, slightly freaked out, I think. "Okay, but there are three videos left." And he made a stupid face which I guess was defensive.

"I mean, during them. If that's not too uncomfortable for you."

"No, I guess not. But I need another shot first. Wait here." Chris rose shakily to his feet and veered out of the room. A few seconds later, he yelled, presumably from the kitchen, "Do you mind if I'm really fucked up? I'll still do what you want."

"Fine," I yelled back.

"Thanks!" I could hear the metallic and scratch-scratching sounds of a shot being readied. "It'll be . . . easier."

The Hispanic boy is gone. Chris is being fucked by the man. The man's eyes are locked on Chris's face, which looks a bit too transported to be on a child. On second thought, maybe he's sort of relieved, since the show's almost over. After thirty, thirty-five seconds, the man yanks out his hard-on. He leans over, fastens his mouth to little Chris's, and comes. Then the visual darkens.

"Hey," I yelled, aiming my voice through the door, down the hall. "You okay?"

Out of the kitchen's slight humming, a very smeared voice, almost unrecognizable, more like a texture, said, "Yeah . . . I'll be . . . there in a . . . minute."

The TV screen blued.

I stood, stretched, and toured the room. Barren walls, thrift-store furniture. By far the most curious, least dusty spot held a smallish bookcase stuffed with kids' storybooks. You know, with those hard, shiny, cartoony covers. I was wondering which one to yank and inspect when a colored light flashed in my peripheral vision.

"Chris!" I listened. "It's starting!"

In the video, Chris, maybe a year or two older, lounges next to a pool wearing small, tight swim trunks. A slightly older boy, around thirteen or so, with a crew cut and skateboarder clothes, tiptoes up with a beer, which he pours over Chris's head. They yell back and forth. Then Chris drags the boy down to the towel and unzips his pants. Chris reaches inside, and they French-kiss.

"Chris," I repeated. "Get your ass in here."

I didn't hear shit. So I took a little trip down the hall. "Oh, Chr-i-i-is."

He was sitting at the table. It was strewn with the same—maybe dirtier—paraphernalia. His eyelids were three-quarters shut, and his mouth was so ajar that his jaw seemed to swing back and forth in a draft.

"Wake up," I said. "Sex time."

"What?" Chris opened his eyes. He was grimacing, I think. "Then, uh . . . help me, all right?" He held out a very limp, dangly arm. "Because I can't . . . I'm, uh . . . too high."

I raised Chris to his feet and steadied him with a hug. That felt so sweet that I maintained it awhile, absorbing the pokes of his pointy bones, his low body heat, and the long-unwashed smell of his hair. But he kept getting heavier and heavier. So I renegotiated our hug and started walking him back to the living room.

Sometimes, when I'm fucking a guy, I want to wind him up, freak him out, make him writhe. Sometimes, I want to do the exact opposite. And with Chris, it was the latter. I wanted him finite, by which I guess I mean dead. But I'm not an evil man, so I did what I do, i.e., hit on a compromise. Chris nodded out, and I explored him as intricately as I could with my tongue, dick, and fingers, and daydreamed insanely until he was gore.

One of my fingers was up Chris's ass. There was this hard rock of shit stuck in there like some horrid antique. I was poking it around. We were lying side by side on the couch. He seemed very far away. Or, should I say, I'd just noticed the distance. "What are you thinking about?" I asked.

"I don't know." He'd been staring at . . . what . . . the TV? By that point it was nothing but a frame with some grayish-white snow in the center.

"Tell me," I said, absentmindedly pinching his nipples. They were already flowery from my twists, pokes, et cetera.

Chris's hand fell on the top of my head. "I don't know," he repeated. He patted me several times. "I'm just so fucked up. I kind of hate it."

"Like how?" And I squeezed a second finger up his asshole. "You mean, the heroin?"

"That," he said. "But not only that. Can I tell you something weird?"

Chris turned onto his side very carefully, then adjusted his head until our eyes were aligned. I've never seen tinier pupils. Still, there was something irregular in them—I mean, apart from his perpetual dazed self-involvement. Whatever it was, it didn't seem to relate to the fingers I'd plugged into his ass, although they must have been affecting his thinking. Technically, I mean.

"I want to die," Chris said. Then his eyes studied mine. "I had this feeling, during the sex, that you knew."

"When?" It sounds strange, but if things get intense in my life, I grow extremely objective, like a journalist.

"I don't remember. You seemed kind of angry."

I'd just worked a third finger into his ass, so most of my thoughts were down there, relaxing in the snugness and heat. "That's so weird," I said. I'd just remembered the moment. We'd been fucking face-to-face, and a detail from one of my violent fantasies slipped out my mouth, and I think I'd said, "Die," very softly. "Yeah, I was imagining killing you."

"I could tell." He looked up at the ceiling, but he might have been thinking of the sky. "Well, I kind of wish you had."

"You shouldn't say that," I said. "It's too amazing."

Chris looked away, squinted at something, then checked back. "Listen, I just . . . oh, fuck." He shut his eyes. "Please."

"Jesus," I said. "Come on." I slid my unoccupied arm around his back, and we hugged for a while. I was very turned on from exploring his ass, so it felt like love, but in this backhanded way,

if that makes any sense. Or it did to me. I mean, I felt totally relaxed, which I almost never feel.

"Think about it," he whispered.

"I did."

"You should kill me."

"I'd get caught." That was sort of a joke.

"I don't care." Chris let out a rough, whistly breath. "Wait
here," he added. Then he carefully eased himself off my fingers,
struggled to his feet, tottered across the room, and shoved one hand
into the bookcase. "Read this." He yanked out a book, turned, and
tossed it.

I skimmed the book. It was three-quarters cartoony pictures and
one-quarter gigantic words, very few of them more than one syl-
lable. A little boy who looked vaguely like Chris lost his way in a
forest. He noticed a cabin and knocked on the door. A man who
looked vaguely like me answered. The man was all friendly at first,
but a few pages later he axed the little boy into millions of pieces.
The pictures made it look magical.

We sat on the couch, reading books. Chris had grabbed about
a dozen and stacked them between us. He was himself again, meaning he looked like an oversize child with unfocused blue eyes.

"They're so violent," I said.

"Mm-hm," he mumbled. He seemed very involved in a story.

The book I was skimming concerned a little boy, maybe
Swiss, who gets cooked in an evil dwarf's oven. "How long have
you wanted to die, if you don't mind my asking?"

"Oh, God," he said, and put down the book. "Since forever.
But it's gotten worse. I think it's the heroin."

"You should quit."

"I know, I know." He reopened the book and tried to bury his eyes in it.

"I'll help you," I said.

Chris wasn't listening. He was back in the book, but he didn't appear to be reading. His eyes looked too starey to take language in. Still, they zigzagged down page after page. "I should have died when I was a kid," he mumbled, and shot me a glance. It was . . . fraught. I don't know how else to describe it. Like he had an idea that was too gargantuan and/or unformulated to pass through such minuscule pupils. "What if it wasn't just you?"

"Meaning?"

"Because there's this other guy." He put the book aside, took a deep breath, lurched off the couch, and stumbled toward the TV. "I just did a porn with him. Tell me if I'm crazy." He ejected the old tape and slotted in a new one.

In the video, Chris is himself. His costar is a small, flabby boy with a humongous dick—who I slowly realize is a dwarf. Chris is flat on his back, nodding out and in, while the dwarf crawls all over him, licking and nibbling his details. At one point the dwarf takes a seat on Chris's chest, leans way over, gets Chris's neck in a tight stranglehold, meets his eyes, and makes an angry or terrified face.

"That guy totally wanted me dead," Chris said. He smiled serenely and pushed his face into the porn, as if the TV screen were a sunlamp.

"This is creepy," I said. "It's like kiddie porn from hell."

"I don't think it would make any difference," Chris continued, still sunning away. "I'll just get old."

"You can't know that."

"If I'd died as a kid, the world would be totally the same. I haven't done shit in my life. I don't even have any friends."

"We're friends."

"Yeah, maybe." He opened his eyes—technically anyway. "But wait, watch this. Look at him. Isn't he just . . . ?"

The dwarf continues to choke Chris as murderously as he can, given the babyishness of his hands and the relative girth of Chris's neck. He still looks upset in some manner that's hard to pinpoint. Chris's face is very bloated and purple, but his eyes are just blissed. And without their disapproval, he does make one's mind wander in scary directions. Or my mind, anyway. But then, I'm sick.

"I need another fix." Chris shot to his feet, which made his knees crack explosively. "Do you mind?"

"What? No, no." I was lost in the porn.

The porn had this strange, silly, magical . . . I don't know, charm. I guess it was mostly the fact that I was watching a dwarf, with all his fairy-tale baggage. Anyway, when he finally unhanded Chris, clutched his dick, gave a few whacks, and came, all I could think was What the fuck?

"Shit," said a voice down the hall.

"You okay?" The porn had just faded to black.

"Yeah." A distant chair creaked. "I have to tell you my fantasy," he yelled. "I keep planning it out in my head." There were some clinks, scrapes. "Sometimes I sit here and think about it and think about it."

"Do tell," I yelled back.

"Okay, shit . . . well . . ."

In Chris's fantasy, he's a ten-year-old lost in some forest. He sees a cabin with sweetly lit windows, and knocks. A monster of some sort invites him inside. As soon as the door shuts, the monster tears Chris's clothes off, ties him down on a bed, and tortures him for hours and hours. Then they fuck, and as the monster comes, he brings out this machete and hacks Chris's head off. That's making a long story short.

"Hey." Chris stumbled through the door and flopped down beside me. He draped one leg over mine. "So what do you think?"

"It sounds like a snuff fairy tale."

"Yeah, of course." He waved at the book pile.

"I mean it's completely unfeasible."

"I guess." Chris yawned, leaned in close, kissed my neck, and laid his head on my shoulder. "But isn't it perfect?" He pecked me again. "Because then the killer and I would be equally happy."

"Maybe for a second or two," I said. "Then you'd just be dead, and he'd be paranoid and guilty for the rest of his life."

"Whatever." Chris's head shifted around on my shoulder. "I'm going to nod for a minute, okay?"

"Sure." I needed some time to reorient, anyhow.

It's strange about junkies. I mean, how they smell. The only other place I've ever smelled that particular odor was once, years ago, when a friend of a friend had an epileptic fit in my living room. But in that case the odor exploded right out of him, and with junkies it's more like a radiance.

"Think about . . . about . . ." Chris swallowed. ". . . how you'd want . . . to do it. Because . . . I'm open."

Actually, I'd just gotten the strangest idea.

In my fantasy, Chris's death wish would be the plot of a porn film. I'd write the script, he'd narrate, and the star would be a boy who resembled the much younger him. Essentially, the porn would re-create the fantasy he'd just related. My logic was: Maybe if Chris's fantasy could be enacted on film, he'd have it to study but he would

still be alive. And, on a purely selfish level, I'd be halfway to literalizing a dream.

"I like mine better," Chris said. He was trying to open his
eyes.

"That dwarf could play the monster."

"Oh, really?" He sat up, blinked. "So . . . wait. I'd be in a fairy
tale, and I'd die, and then . . . the fairy tale would be a film, so I
would still be alive but I could watch myself die for the rest of
my life?"

"Exactly." I hadn't really thought it out this far.

"Hunh." Chris slid a book from the stack. "I want to be him,"
he said, cracking the cover. His finger dropped on a page. It showed
a little blond boy walking into some scrawl of a forest. "Watch."
He turned the page.

The boy walked, it got dark, he saw a cabin, he knocked on
the door. . . .

Chris's face was getting looser, crazier, lost in the plot. I followed along for a while, then the story's predictable twists and turns
lost me, and my eyes trailed off into the wilds of his crotch. It made
me want to wander away from the world. So I did.

"That feels nice." Chris patted my hand, snuggled close, and
shut the book. "So tell me your fantasy again. You know, slowly."

Those were a pretty few minutes. Chris nodded out, and
I daydreamed aloud. And my fantasy, which put a ten-year-old
Chris look-alike through a lyrical nightmare of hot sex and torture, worked its black magic, or became a bizarre fairy tale.
It made me feel like a kid. Or maybe I felt like a parent, because
it wasn't as if the tale itself became real. But Chris did. Or his
story did.

Sunshine Superman

I've been hallucinating for hours off and on. According to the acid, which has just hijacked my mind yet again, I'm standing—or, rather, floating around—on the set of a snuff film in progress. My eyesight's gone quite otherworldly, so it's very hard to say, but that could be Chris tied to a bed. His face is slightly detached from his head, a thin, silvery, masklike hologram of his agonized features, almost translucent, hovering about an inch from where they usually rest. Some guy is bent over Chris, knife out, hacking his genitals off. It only takes a few seconds to free them, but the action keeps repeating, as though it were looped, all in extremely tight close-up. Each time they loosen, the murderer moans, and Chris sucks in a breath. It creates this terse, danceable rhythm. Then it stops. There's a cut or whatever. It's later. The murderer's gone. Chris seems dead. I think that coin-purse-looking lump on the floor is his balls. And there's a lot of other stuff going on, but I couldn't translate it if you paid me. I'm writing this account a few hours after the fact, and my brain's still too fried to go into much detail. That's the one annoying thing about acid. Everything's so complicated and vivid when you're tripping, but language is hopeless at capturing wherever you are, or, in this case, wherever you recently were. Words just dry out. So if this section seems sketchy and half-baked, that's why. But I'm doing my very best, really.

Mason's nose breaks the dream's surface, which ripples out, dims, then eventually dissolves into the lines, sags, et cetera, which years of ironic detachment have imprinted on his face. He's looking me square in the eyes. "Scott and I are leaving," he says, for the third or fourth time, I think. All I really understand is the absence of Luke from that sentence. "Are you back among the living?"

"I'm cool." I am, although, like I said, several seconds before I'd been in virtual reality, watching some figment of my imagination trash the spitting image of someone I . . . I was about to say love, but that's not really true. "Where's Luke?"

"Luke, Luke, Luke," Mason says in this singsongy voice. He's making his "I know you" face. I'm way too fucked up to describe it at the moment. "Luke's going to ask if he can crash here," he adds, overmeaningfully. Then his eyes become two thrift-store-painting-like takes on my emotions re Luke that are so much cheesier than the thing they depict that they're sort of like souvenirs you'd pick up at Niagara Falls or wherever.

"Fuck off." I hear the microwave ping in my kitchen. Because Luke must have caused it, it sounds like God, I swear.

"This was such a mind-fuck," Scott says. I can't quite make him out, but I'd know that whine anywhere. Oh, wait, there he is, across the living room, studying this framed pencil drawing he gave me last year—a pseudo-Japanimation frame which shows Astroboy, Ranma, Speed Racer, and Devilman rimming one another in a daisy chain—which is probably all scratched to shit by shooting-star-like light trails, if my eyesight's anything to go by. "I can't do acid anymore," he continues. "It makes me think art is pathetic, and I can't think art's pathetic, even if it is." Then he looks at

Mason and me for approval, disclaimers. But I'm on acid, so art does seem pathetic, even though it isn't, I'm sure.

Luke enters eating a grilled Swiss cheese sandwich. "Do you mind if I hang around?" he asks.

It's so weird. As soon as Luke entered my peripheral vision, I became happy. And because I'm on acid, I can literally feel and even hear that emotion corrupt my interior. Every atom combusts or whatever. You know, like they're wannabe embers, and my body's a . . . I don't know, fancy-shmancy fireplace or something. Point is, I'm glowing, et cetera.

"That'd be great," I say. And I look into Luke's immense, cartoony eyes with so much love that I feel like my skin offers no personal protection whatsoever.

Luke makes a happy, goofball face and gives the cheese sandwich a lionesque chomp. "I can't believe I'm hungry," he says between chews.

Scott and Mason are grayish, like pieces of the living room that just happen to be able to move.

"You have a cool place," Luke says, looking around. "I've always thought so." He must mean the run-down, eccentric, bread-box-shaped shell that I've crammed with CDs, books, and friends' artwork. It was designed by some Frank Lloyd Wright type in the fifties. The roof leaks, the paint's peeling, but it does look kind of fairy-taleish if you don't have to live here. "The place I'm living is such a hellhole."

"So why don't you move in?" I guess that sounds insane, but frankly, I've been fantasizing for months about asking him to live here.

Luke stops chewing. "Seriously?" he says with his mouth full.

"Yeah."

He swallows. "When?"

"Now. I won't even charge you rent."

"Why not?" He takes another bite.

"I don't know. Because I'm okay financially. And I'd love you to live here."

Mason and Scott are locating their coats or whatever.

"Cool," Luke says, and swallows. "I'll drop my stuff off tomorrow. Not that I have much, just some CDs, clothes, posters . . ." Then he smiles. From what I can gather, the smile means he's happy, and that he can tell I appreciate his happiness, and that he appreciates my appreciation, and that he wants to be appreciated so unbelievably. It feels like love, whether it is or not.

Oh, Mason and Scott leave the house around now, I don't care. Suffice it to say, Mason exudes a sleazy, conspiratorial air that I can't relate to at all. Scott is sullen, wrecked.

I smile at Luke's face, which is still smiling at me. There's something in the air between us that I've never . . . what's the right word? . . . experienced before, or not with this assuredness, and which I have decided to call love, because I want to be loved so unbelievably.

Luke's face is more beautiful than it could possibly be—in the real world, I mean. It's long and rather narrow, with deeply sculpted cheeks, a light spray of freckles, the beginnings of crow's-feet, and a very faint five o'clock shadow. His eyes are huge, greenish-hazel, and engraved with a nervous expression. He has a small, pointy nose, full lips that seem to pout when he's thinking, and big, mismatched ears. He keeps his long brown hair hiked up behind them, though several strands have fallen loose on one side and are jiggling around near his chin, which is square and abrupt, like a broken stalactite.

"How was your trip?" I say, because I have to say something.

"Nice," Luke says. "I spent a lot of time looking at things. Like the parts of the walls that are all cracked and textured. And the rug. The patterns."

"What about the kiddie porn?"

"Yuck," Luke says. "TV's too simplistic when you're tripping. Or it is for me. And things like kiddie porn bore me." He looks away, thinks a bit, pouts. "Can I say that Mason is starting to give me the creeps?"

"Me too. I used to think he and I were extremely alike, but I guess I've changed, or he's changed. Probably both, because . . ."

Luke's losing interest in the topic. He appears to be there, listening closely, but his eyes—or, rather, their beauty—have been refracted elsewhere by his fucked up mind's movement. They're being absorbed by his thoughts, which are probably weighing some personal issue, meaning they've become more and more sublime to think about—to me, anyway. Still, he nods politely. He does this a lot, i.e., moves on mentally. Sometimes I think he's only about a third in the world at any given time. I'm probably the same way, except when he's around. "Do you have any candles?" he asks softly from wherever he is.

"Maybe in the kitchen, why?"

Suddenly he's in the kitchen, digging around in a drawer. He comes back holding two skinny white candles that I can't recall buying. He places them at opposite ends of the coffee table, unzips his backpack, pulls out several sticks of incense, searches the table for wormholes, finds some, and plants the incense. Then he lights everything with a Zippo, blows out the incense, and sits carefully on the couch. "Better," he says. "When I live here, we have to keep a lot of incense and candles around."

"Sure." Whatever he says. I'm so in awe of him, it's fucking scary.

"Cool." His eyes jet to my CD collection. "You're such an indie-rock kind of guy."

"I guess. And you?" The room's filling up with a bitter, flowery smell.

"I guess you'd say my tastes run to techno, but that term is so limiting. But, yeah, ambient, trance, tribal . . ." He shrugs.

"Play me some."

"Will do. Hey, I don't know if you remember, but I tried to find something to play while we were tripping. And your only CDs that are close to my tastes are the Pet Shop Boys and ABBA, and I really like them both, but they would have sounded so wrong on acid. So I decided to get into the silence, and things like the sound of Mason rewinding and fast-forwarding through the video. And it wasn't bad. It gave me some ideas." Suddenly he blinks, which seems to center me back into his consciousness or whatever. "Oh, how was your trip?"

"Heavy," I say. "I spent most of it looking at you. But then I'd go off on these hallucinations where I was just gone."

Luke snorts, I think about the fact that I'd been looking at him. Or, rather, about my announcement of the fact, since he obviously knew I was focused on him. I mean, acid doesn't blind you, or not for very long. "What were the hallucinations like?"

"All over the place," I say. "You know how it is. They're profound in the moment, but if I tried to describe them . . ."

Luke is looking at me, technically, and his head nods at regular intervals, but I can see in his eyes, which have grown almost painfully mysterious, that my voice is a sound track, ambience, and he doesn't really care if it continues or not. When I shut up midthought, feeling fairly embarrassed, he notices, or seems to, and smiles—one of those huge, goofy, sweet, indescribably resonant smiles that are all about his happiness and my obvious appreciation.

"Are you tired?" I ask.

"Yeah," Luke says. "I doubt I can sleep, but I'll give it a try in a minute. Can I use your bed? I mean, you're welcome to sleep there too when you get tired."

"Sure."

"After I trip, I like to sleep next to someone I've tripped with."

"Understandable," I say quickly. "Yeah, that'd be nice."

Okay, this is rough, because it forces me to think about whether I'm into Luke's body. I am, of course, although the acid is making the idea of sex seem really corny and half-thought-out, thank fucking God. Like I've said, I'm trying to keep Luke and sex separated in my mind, not that he'd be interested in fucking me anyway. I'm too old, too easy, too emotionally available . . . I don't know. These are my guesses. We've never broached the subject. Still, self-absorbed as he is, he must find my extreme adoration of him at least vaguely suspicious. Once, maybe twice, we've talked about what types of guys we find attractive. His type bore no resemblance to me whatsoever. But when it was my turn, I described Luke without even thinking. You know, tall, thin, pale, dark hair, big eyes . . . He seemed oblivious to the resemblance, but he must have known. Anyway, I'm in scary territory at the moment and I'd better change subjects. But, yeah, to be perfectly honest, when I'm sitting here alone, and sex comes up, and I pull out my dick and aim it into the realm of remote possibilities, Luke is the file that clicks open.

Luke and I talk for the next, oh, half hour or so, then there's this knock on the door. I want to ignore it, but Luke's curious, and his moods are extremely infectious—to me, anyway. So I go see who's there, and it's Chris. He's visibly jonesing for dope, but there's this . . . I don't know, actual mood in his eyes, as opposed to their usual prickly haze. Poor Chris. Heroin's pretty much eaten him out. Back when we met, he had so much surface. Even when drugs would intermittently do their sadistic little number on his looks, the change intrigued me in a Jekyll and Hyde kind of way. Luckily he has one of those pixieish faces that contextualize wear fairly well. But you have to squint.

"I have to talk to you," he says. "Something really fucked up has happened."

"Shit," I say. "Is it really important? Because I'm on acid, and Luke's here, and we're kind of . . . hanging out."

Luke's name horrifies Chris, I'm pretty sure, but I wouldn't know how to describe how I know. "Yeah, it's important," he says. "*Fuck*, Dennis." His eyes are really digging around in my eyes. Usually they're just organized into a distanced, seductive expression, and frozen there for as long as Chris thinks it will take to get a reaction from me. Really, I could be anyone. If I wasn't so mentally sick, I'd have dumped him months back. Actually, I doubt that, come to think of it. I'm such a wuss. But it's gotten so I fantasize about dumping him every day, and his murder is barely a passing thought, except when I'm loaded, I guess.

"All right, but just for a couple of minutes, okay?"

"Thanks." He's inside.

"Chris is here," I tell Luke as we enter the living room. And I shoot him a look, like, Prepare for the worst.

"Hi," Chris says sharply. He throws himself onto the couch and gives the smoking incense sticks an appalled little glance.

"Hey," Luke says. When he looks at Chris, his eyes become . . . hard, fixed. It isn't disapproval, exactly, more like anxiety mixed with a little . . . I don't know, hunger or something. Word has it he's sort of attracted to Chris, so maybe that's it. In any case, it's the most incongruous look I've ever seen on his face.

"Things are so fucked up," Chris says. He's gazing at me, and shooting Luke these occasional glares. "A kid just died. At Pam's. For no fucking reason at all. He wasn't even that high. I had to get out of there, so I took the bus. Pam told me I could tell you about it, but . . ."

I'm watching Luke, who is clearly alarmed. When he's tense, his eyes enlarge, and his lips stabilize into the aforementioned pout.

He probably hopes this expression is sturdy enough to read as cool and detached. But he's too pure a person, so it doesn't read as anything but self-protective and scared, at least to someone as thrilled by his every emotional minutia as I am.

"You want to crash?" I ask Luke. "I'll talk to Chris for a minute, then join you."

"Yeah." He sort of bolts to his feet.

"I'm sorry," I say very quietly.

"Don't be," Luke says. "See you in a while." Then he veers toward the bedroom. Thanks to the acid, he leaves this long, crooked, translucent trail in the air that's so weird that I space into a staticky trance.

When I wake up, Chris is watching the spot Luke vacated. "Why do you like that dork so much?"

"Luke's the most incredible person I've ever known," I say absentmindedly.

"Oh, come on. In what possible way?"

"It's indefinable. That's the thing about him. It's like a kind of holiness."

"*Please*." Chris's face crumples. "We really have to talk."

"We are."

"Look . . ." He leans forward and scrutinizes my face. Actually, interest in anything other than dope would be very unlike him at this point. So maybe I'm off. In any case, thanks to the acid, I guess, it feels like we're involved in a battle of the brains—or, more specifically, a battle of the drugs in which our minds are the secret headquarters and our eyes are the armies. At first I think I'm completely outmaneuvered, that acid's complexity is no competition for heroin's blissful self-absorption. Then Chris slaps one hand over his eyes, and I figure I've won. Then he throws me a curve. "I'm in love with you, okay?" he says, sounding really pissed off.

Oh shit. "I . . . don't know what to say," I say. Because I don't. "I love you too." But that doesn't feel true when I say it. "And I'm very, very into you physically, you know that." Definitely true, although, like I said, it's a cruder interest than before. "But as much as this thing about killing you fascinates me, I'm sort of—"

"No, no, listen." Chris's hand loosens and flops into his lap. There's nothing new in his eyes—on first glance, at least. "I'm sure now. When I saw that dead kid, I knew." He points at the floor, meaning the dead kid, I guess. "I want to be like that." He points, points, points. "I want to be this thing that fucks with people's heads like that kid did with Pam's. And I want to do it tonight, so I can't change my mind."

Chris's agitation is flushing out my affection for him. I hate how compassion can eat through anything, even acid. "All right, look," I say. "Get off heroin, and if you still want to do it we'll see."

Chris thinks about that and I study him. It's strange what goes on in your head when you're attracted to someone—I mean, so turned on that your thoughts are just a twisted narration to his day-to-day life, and then by some fluke or fated twist or whatever you get the chance to fuck him whenever you want, and you start to realize that his sublimity's just your own imaginative garbage, period, and that all you're going to get out of him is a new set of needs, body odors, opinions, emotions, et cetera, all of which you completely recognize from your other relationships, and you start thinking, So why am I prioritizing him again?

Chris opens his eyes, which crashes my stare. "If you fall in love with Luke," he says, "you'll be sorry."

"That's not an issue, but why?"

"Every time I see you guys together, it's the same," he says. "You radiate worshipful bullshit toward him, and he sucks it up. But there's nothing coming back at you, man. I take advantage of you too, but . . . at least I put out. And unless . . . you guys have started fucking . . ."

"You're misreading the Luke thing," I say.

"You're not fucking him." Chris looks relieved, I think. In the old days I would have ventured a much wilder guess, but like I said, either addiction has demystified him, or I'm not impressed enough with his current thinking process to bother.

"No." I probably should have lied.

Chris fights off a smile. "I should go," he says. "I told Pam I'd help her deal with the kid." He struggles to his feet. Maybe out of habit, I sneak a look at his ass. It fascinates me how when skinny guys stand or sit down, their asses open and close. I love how a pair of old jeans can beautify that activity, sort of the way a river beautifies its bed of rocks and sand. Thing is, at the moment I'm just eyeing Chris's ass out of habit. Maybe I'm thinking how sexy I usually find it. Of course, Chris knows me—or, rather, he knows how my lust operates, so he watches my eyes scrub his jeans, then he gets this weird little prideful half smile that isn't based in reality—on this occasion, at least. "Walk me out," he adds. "I'll make it worth your while."

"Okay." Like I said, sex isn't sexy at the moment, but that doesn't mean it's a boring idea. And Chris is an interesting creature, impaired or not. Really, if my life was a movie, and the sex scenes were edited out, he'd definitely be up for an Academy Award for his strangely sensual, erratic, Gary Oldman–esque performance. It's got all the earmarks.

We walk to the front door, outside, and around to the side of the house, where there's a narrow, woodsy gap between the building and fence. It's dark, and Chris stands there, hands dug deep in his pockets, looking at me with what could definitely be love. It's a strange look—icy, fragile, electric. But that could be a trick of his dilated pupils. "You've got five minutes," he says in this fake hustlery voice that I haven't heard him use in a while. "Whatever you want to do. Then I should go."

I want to comfort Chris, I don't know why. So I hug him, and when he's mine, arms encircling me too, this emotion erupts, although it's more like I feel a chemical being flushed from my brain through my neck and down into my body. It's not love, at least not compared to how I feel about Luke. Empathy's a decent guess. In any case, it's an intriguing sensation. To heighten the effect, I slide one hand down the back of his jeans, and take a gentle handful of his flat, cold, inexplicably mind-blowing ass. That does it. I'm into him—technically, anyway. "You'll be okay."

"Fuck," Chris says into my neck.

It's weird. I'm not remotely turned on. It's more like I'm directing a scene in a porn film. You know, intuiting what would seem steamy with no thought of getting off personally. "If you knew how amazing you were . . ." I say. See, the trick to extracting great sex out of Chris is to grab his ass, moan politely, then introduce a compassionate comment, because he's never gotten much clearcut affection. Normally I do this without even thinking. But acid has altered me into an evil scientist of interpersonal contact—as regards Chris, at least.

Chris's arms tighten around me. "Thanks," he whispers, and kisses my neck. "But I really want to die. It scares the shit out of me, but I do." His hard-on is sawing my pant leg. "I wish I could come," he adds.

"Kick dope and you will." Step two: I work a fingertip into his asshole, which has been fucked so hard so many times in his life that it gobbles me into his body.

"Don't you want to kill me?" he says, and backs over my finger. There's that weird, antique shit. Yuck. "Let's rent a cabin somewhere. Come on, Dennis, you know this is fate."

"It's not that simple, Chris." Maybe it's the acid, but I'm start-ing to feel like he's too good at this. Sex, I mean. Normally I'd be concentrated inside him. When I'm turned on, I can get very reverential about things like that—the perfection of somebody's asshole's design, temperature, whatever. Right now, Chris just seems too eroticized, as if something's haywire in his brain, and the signals that normally flash to his heart or wherever are being misdirected to his crotch. "You should go," I say. "I'm too high to get a hard-on, and I should check in with Luke."

Chris leans back and studies my features. Thanks to the acid, his eyes are just eyes, period. I.e., two moist globes of colorful tis-sue. But nothing on acid's that simple, of course, so I start won-dering what his eyes mean in the grand scheme of things, and from what I can gather, they—or, rather, anyone's eyes—mean . . . well, the answer's beyond me. Let's say they mean chaos. I know that's vague. How to describe it . . . Okay, imagine human eyes are UFOs. I mean, in the sense that their existence proves once and for all that reality's far too complex to be decoded by you. God, I guess I'm pretty high.

Back in the house, I pour myself a glass of cold Sparkletts, and open the bedroom door very, very carefully, in case Luke's asleep. But the light's on, and he's in bed watching me enter.

"Is he gone?" Luke asks.

"Yeah." I sit on the bed's edge, untying my Timberlands.

"That was so weird," he says. "I used to think Chris was cute, but fuck that."

"Chris is a mess, but he means well."

"Whatever." Luke's face . . . scrambles—beneath the surface, I mean. I can literally see one thought fracturing and another thought gradually forming from its remnants. The evidence is subtle, just a few newish crumbs of energy in his eyes, but I know what I'm seeing.

I slide under the covers. I'm pretty sure it's the acid, but as soon as I settle, I have this sensation of being inside something specifically generated by Luke. It's all about warmth, but it doesn't have the huge, impersonal blandness of sunlight, or the detailing and slight insanity of a flickering fireplace, or the clinical heat of a heater, or the wild rush you get plunging into a hot tub. It's a weaker heat, more poetic, and it practically itches. Does that follow?

"So are you guys going out?" Luke asks. He's an amazing foot away.

"Going out," I say, wondering. "Well, it's complicated. We've been sleeping together, yeah, but it's not . . . heavy. He's a junkie, right? And I don't know if you've been around junkies that much, but for them nothing competes with the drug. So I don't know what to call what we do, but I'm trying to end it."

"This is kind of personal," Luke says. "But . . . what do you do?"

At first I don't know what he means. Then I squint at his eyes for a second, decode a little swatch of their beauty, and take a wild guess. "Sexually?"

"*No.*" He means yes.

"Uh . . . Gosh, well, Chris gets incredibly high, and I . . . explore him."

Luke glares at me. "Yes, *and* . . . ?" That's interesting. Oh, sorry. What I'm thinking about is that every time Luke is confronted with something he can't grasp at once, he goes on the mini-attack. On the surface, his tone reminds me of that garish, appalled tone of voice drag queens use to explode their peculiar thoughts into the male-female world. But because in Luke's case these retorts are so random, and so out of kilter with his general sweetness, they read as eruptions, small and contained, and placed in specific locales by his psyche. I guess I should isolate the exact whens, then figure them out individually. Maybe when I'm less high I'll keep a little log. God, I guess I'm spacing. Let's see, what did Luke ask me? Oh, yeah.

"Well, I'm into asses."

"Duh." Luke rolls his eyes. "I've read your books. Or I've started most of them. But I actually did get through one of your novels. No, wait, I didn't finish it either."

"Specifically? Well, this is sort of embarrassing." I look up at the ceiling, but I'm thinking of the sky. "See, Chris has these violent fantasies. And so do I, actually. So we have to be careful when we're having sex, because . . ." I check back with Luke, who's studying my mouth, or its movement.

"Does it bother you that I don't like your books?" he interjects.

First I'm confused by the question. "No, I guess not." Still, to be honest, I've wondered what it means. As Luke has explained, he doesn't understand why anyone would want to write about the subjects my novels recapitulate so automatically. Neither do I, so we're even. But to him, my work's "obvious." It "bores" him. He'll start a book, then, three or four pages in, begin skipping whole sections, scanning for anything he can relate to. He thinks I'm obsessed with personal interaction, and not open enough to the idea that there could be magical forces at work in the world, things that supersede and transcend people's specialized needs for one another. See, Luke's sort of mystical, if you haven't already guessed. To distill several long conversations we've had, he believes that romantic love, sexual desire, friendship, really everything potentially problematic having to do with other people, are just petty side effects of some far more intangible meaning to being alive, and that somewhere in books, movies, music, drugs, nature, there exists a particular way to believe, a mental system that, once successfully decoded and personalized, would organize everyone else into one vast herd of malleable symbols. Not to say he wants Hitleresque powers. In his ideal world, everyone would be wizards of some

sort, and life would be wildly, invisibly crosshatched with magical spells. Still, I think his motivation is simple. He wants what
he wants. And he thinks anything should be possible, no matter
what. And it frustrates him when others' needs are in conflict with
his. Anyway, I'm sort of spacing again. Let's see . . .

"So," I ask. "How's it going with . . . what's his name?"

"You mean, Michael?" Luke smiles deliriously. "I saw him the
other night."

There's this guy Michael, some club kid whom Luke's never
said more than hello to, if that, but who he's convinced posesses
something—knowledge, spiritual foresight, emotional resonance
—that Luke needs to incorporate into his life. I mean, to me it
just sounds like Luke's dying to sleep with the guy, and yeah, when
pushed, he's admitted the guy's awfully cute. Anyway, Luke has
been doing these . . . I don't know, magic rituals? He refuses to
describe them. From what I've been able to gather, these rituals
"bend the universe"—that's his phrase—in such a way as to align
his and Michael's trajectories, causing their needs to coincide. If
it was me, and I found myself powerfully attracted to someone, I'd
just hang around, hoping against hope that this someone would
find me intriguing. To Luke, that's the obvious, boring way to look
at things like love and desire. What I can't decide is if he really is
way ahead of me on these issues, or if he's just elaborately psycho-
logically fucked up, as some of my friends, namely Mason and
Scott, keep insisting.

"So what does this Michael guy do again? Is he an artist, or
does he have a job, or . . . ?"

A laugh's sneaking into Luke's face. "I don't know."

"Things like that aren't important?"

"Not really." Luke smiles knowingly—or it feels knowing.

"So are you doing your . . . uh, magic things to help it along?"

"I've done a ritual or two," Luke says uncomfortably.

"I can't get you to describe them."

"If I did, it would diminish their power," he says. "The idea is to do a ritual, tell no one, then forget you did it. You could do them too, you know."

"How?"

Luke looks exasperated. "Read *Liber Null & Psychonaut*. It's in my backpack."

"Okay."

"But you have to be sure it's something you really want. Like with Michael, I'm just working on getting him interested. I can take it from there. So think of something you're sure you want."

"You mean, right now?"

"Sure." Luke actually looks interested.

"Okay, let me think." Not that I need to. I spend easily half of my life in my head, spaced out, imagining impossibilities. When I'm not lost in daydreams, I'm just sort of clumsily negotiating whatever the world puts in front of me. I wish the real me and the secretive me were united. I wish I could speak in one adequate, coherent voice and make sense. Or should I say, if I were a sane person that's what I'd wish for. But divided in two as I am, everything's subject to compromise. The only wish that both parts of my psyche have ever agreed on is this: I wish that whenever I saw someone I wanted badly enough to befriend, fuck, romance, murder, have a great conversation with, or whatever else, that I could mutter some word and, magically, there'd be an exact replicant of that person whose purpose in life was to accommodate my fascination. Once I'd exhausted my replicant, I'd say another magic word and it would vanish. That way I'd fulfill every fantasy, evil and/or benign, and never impose my fucked-up self on anyone else in the world. The only problem is, I can't explain this to Luke. It sounds too psychotic. So I think of something else. "Okay," I say. "I wish you could be happy and fulfilled all your life." The sentimentality feels out of place in my voice.

Luke clears his throat. "Cool," he says. His face is strangely calm, fixed. The theater of his personality is regrouping backstage or whatever.

"That's my wish," I say, feeling totally blissed.

Luke's eyes glaze for a couple of seconds, then unglaze. "Cool," he repeats.

"Great," I say. Actually, it's more like a croak. It feels like Luke's just said he loves me, and maybe he has. It feels much more true than, say, Chris's "I love you," I don't know why. Luke is easily as complicated as Chris. Maybe that's it. Maybe someone this complicated can't just reduce what he's feeling to language, and if he does, the idea must be stagnant or finished, like a work of art once it's been given a title. But then I'm pretty complicated myself, and I could tell Luke that I love him in a second. Fuck, I don't know.

"There's something very powerful between us," Luke says. Then he yawns. I don't think it means anything, apart from the obvious.

"Amazingly," I say. I must look insane. Really, my face is completely unaccustomed to having to represent happiness.

"I should sleep." Luke yawns again. Then he rolls over. "Sweet dreams," says his voice. That's his favorite phrase. He says it whenever he leaves someone he really likes. So I guess it means "bye."

"You too." That was a little abrupt. Or maybe it's just that I'm not very sleepy. Still, I reach over and flick off the lamp, then lie there watching Luke's hair, neck, and shoulders emerge from the black. For minutes I study them, feeling the faint, totalitarian, internal whir of the acid's decay into whatever lower-brow, speedlike substance it was cut with. At one point Luke, now asleep, rolls over again, and his unconscious face flops down, oh, half a foot from my own.

I don't know why, but when cute guys are stoned or asleep or frozen solid in photos, my imagination feels safe and takes over my thinking. I can't control what comes next, and I hardly even notice the change. Suddenly I'm irrational, although it's not like a physical change. My body's still painfully shy and respectful of whoever's space, but inside . . . well, it's hard to describe. What I'm trying to say is, I catch myself thinking how sweet it would be if Luke opened his eyes, saw the love in my eyes, and his affections were triggered. We'd gaze back and forth long enough to realize that our goals were a match. Then we'd kiss very softly. No tongues or anything. But speed's evil, as regards me at least. So the second our mouths are enmeshed, I get hungry. Luke too. Next thing I know we're French-kissing and wrestling and licking and biting and . . . If I were a sane person, it would be perfect. Being me, things go totally wrong. I have to punch, slap, and kick myself free of the image. You know, like the thought is a rapist. Not just mentally, but physically. I literally jump out of bed, and tip-toe into the living room.

When I need to jerk off, and the image of Luke feels too volatile, I turn to this small clique of fantasy figures, this mental harem of cute understudies whose membership changes from occasion to occasion like an ill-starred rock band's. At the moment my choices are (1) Chris, the old-timer, (2) Goof, (3) Drew Baldwin, whom you'll meet very shortly, (4) Sniffles, that HIV-positive street prostitute, (5) Chris Gentry, guitarist for the English band Menswear, (6) Daniel James, Tinselstool's singer/guitarist, (7) Brad Renfro, actor, and (8) when I really want to spoil myself, Smear's Alex Johns, the most technically beautiful guy in the world, or should I say the most accessible beautiful image right now, thanks to Smear's popularity.

I raid the pile of rock magazines that I keep by the couch, grab the new issue of *Vox*, which has a Smear cover story, and flip through the pages until I find a decent picture of Alex, in this case drunk, shirt askew, holding a beer toward the camera. Then I sprawl on the couch and concentrate on his perfect, hazed face. Next thing I know, he's sitting just to my right. I strip off his trendy clothes, devise a lanky white body, pose it on the rug, shut his eyes, open his mouth, fill him with primitive sounds, dive in, suck his dick, lick his balls, eat out his ass, shove my dick inside, and fuck him very, very hard, all the while licking and biting his shoulders and neck. A knife appears in my hand. I reach underneath him, place its point to his chest, and tell him he's going to die, to which he makes some agreeable noise. I bury the blade, then drag it down to his groin. When his guts topple out, I shoot my load in his ass, which in turn makes me come on my hand—in the real world, I mean. Orgasms on speed feel so cheap. It's like a sputter. Then I hobble into the bathroom, wipe myself off, flush, and return to the couch. That's better.

In the weird afterglow, I absentmindedly hoist Luke's backpack into my lap, unzip the top, and watch my hand flop around in the deep, lumpy tide pool of rave fliers, tarot cards, sage bundles, cassettes, drug paraphernalia, and so on, until I find the aforementioned book, *Liber Null & Psychonaut*, by one Peter S. Carroll. I page around, feeling cowed by its biblical tone, until I find a longish chapter on magic rituals.

From what I can glean in my speed-read, there are several ways to perform rituals, the most interesting involving this thing called a sigil, which is an emblem made up of letters drawn one on top of another, then enclosed within a circle, so that all one sees is a pattern that looks like an extremely busy logo. Apparently you're supposed to reduce what you want to a sentence— say, "I want to be rich," or "I want so-and-so to fall in love with me"—then build the aforementioned logo out of its letters. Once you've devised an acceptable logo, you stare at it, either in some sort of meditative state or during masturbation, and the meaning behind the logo lodges itself in your thoughts. Somehow, because of your intense concentration or something, a magical process is triggered, and the wish enters reality, viruslike, then fucks with the order of the universe, and you get what you want. Something like that. Supposedly one can devise one's own sigilesque thing, then take the basic principle of the sigil and run. Thanks to the acid, I'm sure, it sounds half-plausible—or charismatic, at least. So I space out around the idea that the alphabet's just a collection of secretive forms, i.e., Aladdin's lampettes. That would explain some of history's eerier twists. I mean, if you factored in magical tweaks. Then I remember what I do when I'm not stoned. You know, write novels that are essentially long, involved wishes for offbeat utopian worlds that I can't realistically enter. And within a few seconds I have this idea, which, if it's not obvious, involves writing a novel/sigil that has a wish neatly embedded inside it. I guess it can't hurt.

I move to my laptop computer, which, like Scott's and Mason's worktables, is isolated away in a small half bedroom that I use as an office. First I pull out a blank piece of paper and think for a second. Then I write down the one thing I'd wish for if wishes could actually be granted. I can't reveal it to you, because that would interfere with the mystical process or something. Anyway, it's not the wish you'd expect, if that helps. I thumbtack the page to the bulletin board over my desk. Then I stare at the wish for a while. Then magically or whatever, I start writing a novel. I begin by describing exactly what's happened to me since I snapped myself out of the heaviest part of the LSD trip. In other words, I start here—or, rather, a dozen or so pages back. That's where everything begins.

Blur

Luke's asleep in my bedroom. I'm at the laptop, milking the speedy tail end of the acid trip. Mason's home making art. So's Scott. Robert and Tracy are filed away inside freezing-cold, human-size drawers. You can basically forget them. Chris just arrived at Pam's studio. He's shooting dope in her office. Pam's a wreck. Goof's right where we left him. His skin's stiffening up like some tiny, wintry lake. Death's so complex.

Mason tore Alex Johns's face from *Select* magazine.

In the boom box, a Sebadoh compilation tape. Turned low, it helped maintain Mason's mood, which was typically grim, detached, horny.

In the shot, Alex was grinning at Graham, Smear's guitarist. In the collage, he'll be imagining Mason's dick. Oh, he wants it. Yeah, right.

The phone rang three times. The machine picked up. It was Scott. He sounded weird, so Mason snagged the receiver.

†

Scott's at his worktable. Until a few minutes ago, he was drawing. His art utilizes a clean, pseudo-comic-book style to deconstruct his psychological makeup. It's mildly entertaining, over-intellectualized, and slightly obscure, just like him. At the moment his drawing pad holds a partly complete comic strip—or, rather, "comic strip." The main character, a waifish androgyne with hippie togs, nervous mannerisms, and mild psychic powers, is modeled on Luke. In the comic, Luke is battling one of those de rigueur insectlike monsters of Japanimation. The monster's supposed to represent Luke's inner child or whatever. And the whole piece is really about Scott's subconscious desires. So it's a little incoherent.

"Did you *hear?*" squeaked Scott's voice. "Robert and Tracy are *dead*, man. In a car accident, on their way home from the Whisky last night."

Sebadoh: Divide the time / The sky misfiring.

"That's weird," Mason said absentmindedly. "What about our junkie friend?" He had this slight thing for Chris's appearance.

Sebadoh: Thing twirls / Hang it out the window.

"He wasn't there," said Scott's voice. "So . . . what does it make you feel? Because I don't know what I feel."

Robert and Tracy were found by the police. The van they'd smashed into had flipped over several times, killing both occupants, a retired gardener and his ten-year-old son. Because of Robert's tracks and the inordinate level of dope in his blood, it was assumed he'd nodded out at the wheel. That's what would now be believed. So it was hard to know what to feel, since we'd already distanced ourselves from the duo, whom heroin had rendered remote, inauthentic, and wildly dishonest. I'd stopped returning their calls months before, for reasons I'll try to explain very shortly.

Anyway, Scott was shocked by the news, and Mason too, though a little less obviously.

Mason pushed SPEAKERPHONE, called me. Using the tip of one finger, he moved the Alex picture around on a blank sheet of paper. "Did you hear?" he asked.

"Yeah," says my voice. "If you mean about Robert and Tracy. And you heard about Goof? You know, that kiddie porn star we like so much? He dropped dead at Pam's place last night."

"What?!" Mason lifted his finger off Alex. "You're kidding."

To Mason, a particular sort of male beauty is everything. It doesn't exist in the world, but certain young actors and rock stars come reasonably close. Hence his art, which collages together extraordinary scraps of human matter—say, Alex's face, Brad Renfro's chest, James Duval's stomach, various porn stars' genitalia, Goof's ass, Leonardo DiCaprio's legs, et cetera—each body part carefully ripped from a photo or magazine, then glued down on a white sheet of paper and aligned with complementary fragments in painstakingly casual, Frankenstein-ish constellations. It's instinctive stuff. He can explain it in theoretical terms, but it's completely obsessive. Luckily for him, obsessive gay art is very trendy at the moment, so he makes a decent living. But his art's just about his own loneliness, period, whether collectors and critics understand that or not. He's building imaginary lovers, friends, sons, younger brothers, slaves, gods. It's a vaguely creepy thing, and it means a fucking ton to him, unlike his actual friends and acquaintances.

Mason yanked out a file drawer and flipped through the folder marked "Beauty." He found, removed a thin deck of Goof Polaroids. He'd snapped them off my TV screen several weeks back.

Them: (1) Goof's face in mock ecstasy. (2) Goof's body squashed to a sickly white stripe by an obese older body. (3) Goof's tiny ass stuffed with a Satanic face. (4) Goof's face in wide-eyed, lower-lip-biting pain. (5) . . .

Plucking the Goof-as-stripe shot, which had this nice painterly quality, he pinned it to the page and moved it here, there, steered by a mysterious Ouija-like force.

Sebadoh: I don't care if nothing else goes my way all day.

The evening Pam lent me that kiddie porn tape, Mason and I held a mini-premiere in my living room. As I recall, we were similarly awestruck, turned on, and a little confused by our hard-ons. Like me, he'd half-wondered what it would be like to have sex with some underage kid. In fact, we both had this slightly discomfiting thing . for Brad Renfro, the teenage costar of a stupid AIDS film called *The Cure*. But when we'd cast very young boys in our fantasies, there'd been no chemistry whatsoever. Actually, I should speak for myself. For me, it had something to do with the scale of their bodies. The things lacked . . . well, I'm not quite sure. Everything was too close together and sort of insufficiently lived-in. And no matter how I tormented or worshiped a boy, I couldn't seem to excite him. He'd just seem sad, scared, upset. Obviously the snag lay in my imagination, since the men in the kiddie porn tape had no problem whatsoever with the size differential. Of course, it helped that everyone seemed so stoned.

I'm in my office, typing a draft of the previous chapter. Several minutes ago, I pushed PLAY on my boom box.

Blur: I met him in a crowded room / Where people go to drink away their gloom.

The office is smallish and barren, apart from my desk, a file cabinet, a filthy Macintosh laptop, and a bulletin board pinned with pictures of people whose beauty inspires me for whatever reason.

On the bulletin board, left to right: Smear crouched in a corn-field, a close-up of Menswear's Chris Gentry, Brad Renfro in swim trunks, Tinselstool's Daniel James making a goofy face . . .

Two weeks after our kiddie porn festival, I stopped by Mason's one night. He sat me down, fed the VCR, and, click, there he was fucking Drew Baldwin, the teenage son of a local art collector. Apparently, Mason had hidden his videocam in a pile of dirty laun-dry. Point is, I was torn. On the one hand, I had Mason dupe me a copy. On the other hand, I was so horrified by Mason's act that I phoned Drew the following day to confess and console him. I thought the tape's existence would freak the kid out, but apart from a few "wows," he basically wanted to know if it made him look dorky or not. Anyway, we had the first of what became dozens of long, involved talks about intergenerational sex, which it turns out he's totally into. Weird kid.

"Wake up, Chris." Pam poked, poked. She was weighing a gnarly idea. "I'm counting to five, then I give you a salt shot. One . . . two . . ."

Chris had nodded out at her desk. "Yeah, yeah," he mumbled.

Guided by Voices: Are you the person I'm scheduled to meet / To assess my skeleton's worth?

Pam leaned in close to his ear. "I have an idea," she said. "Take off your clothes, and go stand next to Goof."

Pam's idea: If Goof's hair was dyed blond, he could pass for a much younger Chris. I.e., he'd make a decent stunt child for the violent scenes in our collaborative project. Light Goof mysteri-ously, face him away from the camera, and he could appear half-alive—meaning, drugged or unconscious. He could be tortured, mutilated, dismembered, et cetera, and thereby spare Pam the expense and/or hassle of faking such things. There was a huge moral issue involved, naturally, but first things first. And she explained this to Chris, who was too high and envious and shocked or whatever to respond complicatedly. Then Pam phoned me.

"Hi, Pam," I whisper, so as not to disturb you-know-who. "What's going on?" I'm up to the part in the chapter where Luke goes to bed.

Blur: No one here is alone / Satellites in every home.

"Listen," said Pam's voice. "About our project . . . I know this is jumping the gun, but would you mind if I shot one of the sex scenes today?"

"I guess not," I say, half-listening. "Why?" Then I cringe while she explains her idea.

I know the Pam, Goof, and Chris story line is preposterous. But I'm in this dilemma. I'm still fascinated by kiddie porn, snuff, and so on, but I want to diminish their presence in my thoughts and, consequently, in my work. And the only way I can think to remove them is through a kind of gentrification, since I guess they still have to be here, as long as I can't keep them out, which I obviously can't. I've tried. What I want here is nothing but Luke and me lost in mutual affection. That's what you'd be reading if I wasn't so deeply fucked up.

Alex, Smear's bass player, opens his eyes. Oh, yeah, hotel. They're wrecked from the post-gig festivities. "Bloody hell," he says.

Across the room, Damon, Smear's singer, is watching TV. He's a scrappy young blond with a cynical mind and huge, technically innocent eyes. "We have an interview out by the pool in an hour." He points at the screen. "Look at this bollocks."

MTV: Some long-haired grunge band stomps around in a strobe-lit graveyard, singing heroin's praises.

Alex sits up. "I need a pack of fags," he says, throwing off the covers. "Want anything?"

Alex, twenty-eight, is an insecure, self-involved, artsy borderline alcoholic with a blandly witty manner, passable musical talents, amazing luck, and this humongous IQ that he exercises only on occasion. Thing is, he's cute beyond belief, if you're into that type. Until the age of eleven or so he was a pudgy math nerd with thick glasses. Then he grew three feet, thinned, styled his hair, found a look, switched to contacts. Now he's sublime—on the surface, at least. It has something to do with his modelesque features, and how they're so thrown out of whack by his odd personality, and how unsuccessfully he has adopted a snooty demeanor to try to seem cool. Anyway, he makes a smallish segment of the rock music audience lose their shit, sexually.

Pam was comparing Goof's ass, genitalia, and nipples to Chris's. "Christ," she joked. "Its dick's bigger than yours."

"*Fuck you,*" Chris yelled. He knocked down a couple of light stands. "This is fucking *hard* for me."

"Look," she yelled back. "All of this shit is for *you*, you stupid junkie. If you'd just—" The rest was drowned by the doorbell.

"What fucking *now*?" Chris staggered to the door, put his eye to the spy hole. "It's your girlfriend," he said, and automatically unlocked the door.

Back in the comic, Luke's proving no match for the monster. With each frame Luke just becomes cuter and more ineffectual, and the monster grows more hideous and omniscient. There's a reason for this, if you're curious. In the real world, Scott's torn between envying Luke's naive faith in the power of magic and thinking the boy needs some serious therapy. And he's pissed at himself for caring what Luke believes. And most important, Scott's into Luke on a sexual level. All that's in his comic somewhere. Plus, I'm sure there's other stuff Scott can't begin to acknowledge and, consequently, stuff I can't begin to describe.

Scott laid down his pencil and shook out some early arthritis.
On the radio, a strangely good song by the Lemonheads, whom Scott normally hates or, more specifically, thinks could be up with the indie-rock gods, i.e., Pavement, Guided by Voices and Sebadoh, if they cared a little less about fame.
Scott's thoughts, in summary: Maybe I'm jealous.
The Lemonheads: Mark my path / Mark my path down.

Love's never been easy for me, especially when there's sex in the mix. My best relationships have almost always involved an unspoken, fierce sexual tension and/or an attachment I couldn't explain except in vague, spiritual terms. I've always loved people younger than me, often significantly so. Paul, whom I'll tell you about very shortly, is a perfect example of the former. Luke must be the ultimate example of the latter. But my actual lovers—guys I've committed myself to emotionally and sexually, and who have desired or loved me in return—are these incredible blurs, like long-forgotten drug highs. What we went through together was far too intense, self-incriminating, and confused to rethink, much less put into words.

Alex walks into the daylight. To the hotel's west, whitish glare. To the east, a line of garishly painted storefronts with trendy names like Cyberia, Web Pagers . . .

His outfit: a red Elastica T-shirt with slightly rank armpits; eggshell white boxer shorts; baggy black jeans sans belt; scuffed brown loafers, no socks.

Heading east, he sticks his head into store after store. Crap, crap, crap . . . Then he hears his name. Somewhere over his shoulder.

"Hi, uh . . ." said a thin, fey man carrying a six-pack of Pepsi. Unfortunately or fortunately, it was Mason. "I . . . liked your show last night."

When I fall in love, it's extreme. I don't fall that often. In most cases, people unnerve me. Love tends to decimate my slightly distant and flaky persona. I become warm, awestruck, there, devoted, and selfless—so much so that it frightens and pisses off people I know but don't love—meaning, most of my acquaintances and friends—because I deprioritize them to such an obvious degree, quit returning their calls, act distracted around them, et cetera. But the high is so great that it's worth losing comrades.

Mason was so tense his voice sounded English. Maybe that's why he seemed trustworthy. "Are you . . . staying near here?"

Alex approaches. Even in sandblasty daylight, his beauty is almost inhuman. "Just up the road. Listen, mate, you wouldn't have a spare pack of fags?"

"I think I might, actually," Mason said. "Look, I live right here." He pointed up at a second-floor window. "Come on in for a second."

When I was thirty, a friend threw a party to celebrate the publication of one of my books. Midway through the evening, this boy wandered in and immediately joined a few chums in one corner. He was so beautiful that my eyes whited out. I had to grab an acquaintance's elbow to stay on my feet. In retrospect, he looked a lot like Smear's Alex, with a suave, childlike face, devilish eyes, straight black hair chopped off just below the earlobes, and a slight, curvaceous body. We cruised each other for a while, then he left. The party's host, noting my interest, rushed over and filled in some details. Paul was an art student, twenty, into slightly older men, and currently unattached. The host said he'd phone Paul the following day and suss out the boy's sexual tastes. The next afternoon, my host called me excitedly. Paul loved my work, thought I was handsome, and we were all getting together for drinks late that night, if I was free.

"Jesus, Pam." Sue had a newly shaved head, a nose pierce, and a boa constrictor tattoo that encircled her neck several times. "Get a grip, baby. This is insane."

Guided by Voices: Send in striped white jets / In through stained-glass ceilings.

Pam tried to talk, but this sob kept exploding the ends of her sentences.

"And you," Sue said. She kicked Chris's wobbly ass. "Get your junkie ass out of my baby's life. Now."

After a few drinks, the host faked a personal crisis and left us alone in the bar. Paul was a bright boy, extremely vain, a bit tense and removed, with a soft, queeny voice that hesitated and wandered from topic to topic, undermined by his need to be loved or whatever. I'm excellent with people like that, so I had no trouble taking him home, although by the time we arrived we were too sloshed to do anything. He had to leave early for school the next day, but we agreed to start dating. When we finally had sex, it was parochial to say the least. Like, Paul insisted we wear our underwear the whole time. Apparently he'd been wooed, fucked once, and dumped quite a lot in his life, so he was sort of mother hen–ish about his dick, balls, and ass. Still, based on what I'd "accidentally" felt through the cotton, they seemed worth the wait.

Alone in the kitchen, Mason opened two Pepsis. Into one, he dropped several Rohypnols, then swirled the can.

"Ta," Alex says when Mason hands him the soda. He glugs some. "Are these yours?" He walks to the wall where Mason's thumbtacked some artwork.

"Things in progress," said Mason. He was studying the seat of Alex's pants. It was like looking at a rock pile and trying to imagine an avalanche.

One night, Paul asked if we could stop having sex altogether. When I got huffy, he burst into tears and told me stories of how he'd been sexually abused—things he'd never told anyone, et cetera. What he wanted more than anything else in the world was to be loved for himself, not just for his looks, and I cared enough about him that I agreed to a deep, primary, platonic relationship. Still, my attraction to him was severe, and repressing it made the desire go ballistic. Behaviorally, I was a saint. But when Paul wasn't looking, I'd study his clothing, eyes peeled for the curve of an ass cheek, the eddy around a nipple, the bump of his dick. I got to be sort of a junkie. I tracked down his ex-lovers, got them drunk, clicked on a concealed tape recorder, and made them tell me every detail. I swiped his briefs, plucked his stray pubic hairs from the rim of my toilet, gathered cigarette butts, et cetera, and organized everything into small Ziploc bags which I labeled accordingly. I still have them in storage somewhere. I really should throw those out.

Scott filled in a frame. First he drew Luke in a comical, boxeresque stance. Then he encased the character in a gloomy industrial landscape.

Caption: And so the boy's magical powers were put to the test.

For whatever reason, Scott filled the next frame with a close-up of Luke's baggy jeans, specifically the crotch, not that anything showed.

Caption: If only he'd known what the monster was secretly after.

Rendering the chaotic ebb and flow of the denim, Scott got a hard-on. He was too busy being an artist to care, but it shifted the comic.

I mention Paul to emphasize how divided I am. And I bring that up again to introduce my dilemma regarding young Drew. We've become really close on the phone, flirtatious, chatty, and sort of scarily honest with each other. He knows I'm fascinated by kiddie porn. And that I think he's incredibly cute. And I know he's into much older men. And that he's sort of into me. Anyway, after putting him off for as long as I could, he's coming over tomorrow to hang out and look at that tape. I'm almost sure he sees this as a date. He's said as much. I don't know what I'm imagining. Or should I say I've discouraged his crush in this roundabout way that accidentally on purpose leaves open the remote possibility that something might happen just in case . . . God, I'm so fucked up.

Pam dropped to her knees. "Listen to me," she said. "I was filming Chris and Goof, and the kid just dropped dead. That's it."

"So Chris shot him up," Sue whispered. And she glared at Chris, who was standing over Goof, making a giant decision. "Don't be naive, Pam. Junkies are evil incarnate."

Guided by Voices: This is not a vacation / There is no place to go.

"I guess," Pam said. She tried to sneak Chris a meaningful wince. "Yeah, I guess that's what happened."

†

I tend to get into things I can't handle. Take Sniffles, one of the kids I wrote about in that *Spin* article. I'm still not quite ready to access the details, but for the moment, suffice it to say that the moral of that little story is: Given the right drugs, the wrong boy, the wrong mood, et cetera, I'm perfectly capable of evil, if such a thing exists. Like I said before, Sniffles's trip was to be trashed during sex. Beating the shit out of boys isn't one of my things, but I guess it was close to the murderous fantasies I had repressed around Chris, because I lost it. I literally had to throw myself off the bed at one point to keep from bashing his head in. Not that he knew or cared or anything. He just thought I was totally wild.

I should really call Sniffles and see how he's doing. It's been way, way too long. Unfortunately, tracking him down means a brief conversation with . . .

"Covenant House," said a sugary voice. "Jeffrey Hitchcock speaking."

"Hey, man," I say. "What's up? It's Dennis. Look, I need to reach Sniffles."

"Ah, yes, our delicious young punk friend," said Jeffrey. Ugh. "Mm . . . I think I might just have a fax number. Let . . . me . . . check."

First I have to hear about Jeffrey's new "client," a preteen illegal alien named Flaco who must be somewhere within earshot, since Jeffrey describes the poor kid in this ludicrous, pseudo-Shakespearean sonnetlike language that he adopts when there's a fuckable boy in his presence. I.e., how the youth's loins beckon kisses like a flower does bees or whatever. It astonishes me that kids fall for that shit, but I suppose Jeffrey's nauseatingly stylized behavior could read as fairy-tale-esque if a kid were just nerdy enough and extremely attention-starved. Anyway, Jeffrey eventually gives me the number of a local AIDS hospice. Then I hang up, scribble a letter asking Sniffles to call me, and fax it. Almost the second I drop the receiver, the phone rings.

"You're there," Mason said. His voice had this . . . twist. It rang a weird bell. "So listen. You should come by. Right now."

"Luke's here," I whisper. Last time Mason's voice had that twist, I dropped by and he showed me the Drew tape.

Blur: We like to sing along / Although the words are wrong.

"So what?" Mason said. "Make some excuse. This is . . . well, let's just say it's important." Then there was the time . . .

Mason strolled back to his studio. Alex had slumped to the floor. From the noisiness of his breathing, Mason could tell that the nap had turned serious. Mason coughed, poked the pop star's arm, pulled a little hair. When he was positive Alex was soundproofed, Mason programmed his boom box to play Smear's "Far Up" for the rest of eternity. It was the only song in the band's catalog that featured Alex's lackadaisical vocals. Then Mason knelt, separated the boy from the half-empty Pepsi, loosened his belt, eased him onto his stomach, relieved him of his wallet, and started digging around in the seat of his baggy black jeans.

Pam dragged Goof out the emergency exit. He was light, loose, a breeze, a broom. His soles left pale, crumbly, eraserlike trails across the parking lot.

Sue cracked the car trunk. She cast her eyes into the afternoon smog. When she heard the thud, she immediately slammed the trunk shut.

Pam squeezed into the passenger seat. "Head downtown," she sniffed. Slam. "There's this lot just off Seventh Street, down by the railroad tracks."

Wait. Someone loved Goof—or, rather, someone loved Nicholas Klein. There's this guy who'll feel old-fashioned pain if he ever finds out what became of the kid. Two years ago, Nicholas crashed for a month at the home of Franz Holt, a well-connected if slightly insane pedophile. To Franz, fucking an eight-year-old kid was pretty much the sublime, so he moved Nicholas in, gave him stuff, paid the bills, investigated adoption proceedings. Nicholas liked Franz okay, but he preferred getting stoned. Thing is, Franz hated potheads. He thought they were evil. Maybe when he was a kid, one had murdered his dog. Anyway, he laid down the law about drugs. Nicholas, who had this irrational fear of sobriety, told Franz to fuck off and split. At the time, Franz was sort of relieved, but as bizarre as it sounds, he's never met anyone half as cute since. Now he could shoot himself.

Frame 7: Luke's eye in tight close-up. It's a crisp oval, quickly blacked in, blurrily reflecting the monster's . . . horny, slobbering face?
Caption: "What's wrong? My powers have failed me."
Scott: Scratch scratch scratch scratch scratch . . .
Frame 8: Luke's crotch, extreme close-up, his dick vaguely outlined amid the general crinkling.
Caption: "What in the world does it want from me? Think, think."

All the beauty in my world is either sleeping, unconscious, or dead. Luke, Goof, Chris, Alex. Life's a scary place without them. All that's left are the artists, the users, the interpreters. Us. Mason, Scott, Pam, Sue, and myself. We're so imaginative and lonely, and their immobility is such an inspiration for some unknown reason. The balance of power is totally off. Maybe I should qualify that. I'm a traitor, okay? I'm making this narrative safe for Luke's character, whatever that takes. I don't care whom I destroy along the way. I only wish I could do the same thing in the less malleable life we're beginning to share.

Mason's apartment is a roadside museum of dusty, curled posters of third-rate rock bands with angelic lead singers. "What the fuck's up?" I say.

"I want your opinion on something," he said, cracking the studio door. "I'm trying my hand at a new medium."

Smear: Silent in the fly at light / Out into the Silky Bay.

"No way." I take a few staggery steps toward the body. I can't count the times we've half-jokingly wished for this exact situation. "How the hell did you—?"

Mason's story: He was on his way home from the 7-Eleven. He saw Alex walking along, looking rather confused. They cruised each other, believe it or not. Mason invited him up. They talked for a while. Sex was definitely in the cards. Alex requested drugs. All Mason had was this bottle of mood equalizers that he'd been prescribed for suicidal depression. Alex swallowed a few. They got naked, made out. Mason told him about me and sort of suggested a three-way. Alex was into the plan. Mason walked into the living room, phoned me, and by the time he came back, Alex had passed out in this very spot and position. About that time I arrived, and . . . Ta-da. Obviously that's 99 percent bullshit. Still, it's astonishing what you'll believe when you want to believe in something badly enough.

†

Chris unfolded a wee scrap of paper. It was practically lint. He flattened it out on Pam's desk. There were tiny blue markings in its tender little craw.

"Hello," said a scrunched, weasly voice. It gave Chris a quick, useless, influential semi-boner.

"This is Chris. We made a porno together last year. Anyway, shit . . . do you feel like killing me? I mean right now."

"Okay, sure." The dwarf was trying to remember. Blond? "I'll spring for a cab." Then he squeaked out direct— "Wait. Did you say . . . 'kill'?"

The dwarf, a.k.a. Don Haggarty, is a stunted, prematurely decrepit twenty-something-year-old with a dwindling trust fund and a nasty degenerative disease. Not that he was ever humongous and cute. Thank God for the fetish porn market, because he works steadily enough to pay huge doctors' bills. This dwarf will fuck anything. Kids, dogs, fat guys, paraplegics. Scat, S&M . . . he's game. He's even got his own line of specialty videos, *Terrible Tales of the Dwarf*. They've been profiled in nonporno contexts like *Artforum, Sight and Sound,* and the like. Their ugliness is a social critique, to some ways of thinking. Thing is, who cares? The dwarf's not complex anymore, if he ever was. It's probably the pain. Anyway, if some fucked-up young guy wants to help him enlarge his repertoire . . . Still, it's all speculation until Chris actually walks in the door. Then when the dwarf gets a load of his victim, well, it makes all the difference in the world. Oh, him.

Smear: My tie in the light sty, won't cry? / Steeply my lamb I snore away . . .

Mason is sculpting Smear's bass player into a slut. We're talking facedown, legs splayed, mouth and ass crack wide open, fists balled at his sides.

Alex: kkhdfflppw . . .

"Okay, I'll leave you two alone," Mason said. He stood, checked his watch. "Half hour tops. And don't muck him up."

From the neck down, Alex is just sort of there. His body's so plain that you'd think he was born wearing clothes. Really, as if God or whoever was working on deadline, and so much time was spent molding the ultimate head that the other three fourths of him had to be built in a hurry. Problem is, I'm also describing my type. There's just nothing like stripping some cute fashion plate and discovering a thin, pale, weirdly proportioned young dweeb underneath. I love how guys like that lose their cool, hunch over, cover their dicks, and hobble into my arms. It's such a huge transformation. It can seem like the greatest magic trick in the world—in the moment, at least. Or should I say, it makes me feel all-powerful, which is hot.

Chris was stripping midroom in this slow, messy, junkie-esque way. It looked hot—to the dwarf, anyhow.

"Let's pretend I'm a kid," Chris said. "And . . . I got lost in a forest and knocked on your door. And you've decided to kill me because . . . okay, don't get offended, but . . . because you hate beautiful people."

"Fair enough," said the dwarf. That was pretty much the story here anyway. "And you promise that nobody knows where you are."

"Nobody knows," Chris said. "And nobody cares. Cross my heart."

Photographs don't do Smear's bass player justice. When I saw the band live, it was heavy. I had to grab Mason's elbow. I fantasized

I was ravishing Alex the whole time Smear played, including several encores. Why him? He must resemble some boy I had a crush
on in sixth grade or something. Isn't that the current thinking on
how beauty works? That it tweaks memory? It's so different from
how I feel looking at Luke, whose beauty is less fixed, less archi-
tectural, and more the result of some ulterior spirit or force that
just happens to mesh perfectly with his sweet, nervous, gawky
persona. Anyway, that's why the Luke character isn't sprawled on
Mason's floor. Or flopping around in the trunk of Pam's car. Or
hanging around at the dwarf's, for that matter. Just on a technical
level, it wouldn't make sense.

Goof ended up on a huge, oil-stained, Texas-shaped scrap of
cardboard.

Pam looked this way, that way. Nothing, nothing. Oh, railroad tracks, Sue's car, a distant homeless encampment . . .

Car radio: I know you think you're deep, all right / But you
should stay in the shallow end.

"I wish . . ." Pam said. She was speaking to Goof, meaning
death, meaning her own imagination. ". . . that you'd had a better
life than you did. I—"

"Pam," yelled Sue's voice. "There's a car coming. We've got
to get out of here. *Now.*"

I know this amazing mental trick. When I come across someone
I'd love to have sex with, then murder, I close my eyes and imagine I'm inside his skin. Then I make him/myself walk around, strip,
shower, jerk off, take a shit, piss. It almost always disempowers his
beauty, humanizes it, gives it this nonchalance, this invisibility,
and connects it to my own set of bodily concerns, which are mostly
organized around issues of maintenance. Here's a perfect example:
Thanks to the aforementioned daydream, I haven't laid a finger

on Alex. Granted, I may regret holding back for the rest of my
life, but at the risk of sounding overly therapy-damaged or something, I'm so proud of myself that when Mason checks up on me
ten minutes early, I wave him inside.

Frame 11: The monster has torn away Luke's hippie clothes.
They're rags fluttering in its baroque, candelabra-like claws.
Caption: The boy accepted defeat by denying that it was
occurring.
Scott: Scratch scratch scratch scratch scratch . . .
Frame 12: The monster is down on its knees, its vast, shim-
mering, broochlike face inches away from Luke's cutesy-wootsy dick.
Caption: "This isn't happening. This isn't happening."

Chris peed. He used the dwarf's Norelco on his pits, crotch, legs,
sideburns. He mussed up his hair. Cool. He kissed his mirror image goodbye. When he emerged, newly kidlike, the dwarf and he
improvised an absurd little scene that established the fairy-tale narrative. The dwarf steered them into the kitchen. Maybe Chris was
overacting a bit, because at one point the dwarf slapped his face
for no reason at all. Chris pretended to cry. When he wouldn't or
couldn't stop crying, the dwarf grabbed a knife off the counter and
stuck it in Chris. Nothing fatal. Still, the pain was a shock. It ruined Chris's concentration, but . . . oh, well. He dropped to his
knees, really screaming. When he wouldn't or couldn't shut up,
the dwarf stabbed him a half dozen times. Chest, stomach, back.
He fell backward. Things were way, way off game plan, but . . . oh,
well. The world was becoming so dreamlike that Chris didn't need
to reopen his eyes. But then he felt something down in his crotch
that was incomprehensible.

†

"Fuck. Oh, *fuck.*" Chris forced his eyes open a slit. His testicles were resting three feet away, in the dwarf's tiny palm. He tried to get into their primitive beauty.

"Shut up." The dwarf stabbed Chris's thigh. He was trying to grasp death's complexity or something.

Chris's shock was so dense and complex that it collided with the world's very different complexity, sort of like what happens when a very strong light hits a very big jewel.

This part's almost over. It has to be gross, a touch abstract, and relatively implausible. Otherwise I'll get too emotionally involved. If it's any consolation, Chris is in pain, period. That's the thing. Without the imagination's elaborate input, dying's no different from breaking your leg. And Chris's mind is too busy sedating his wounds to contemplate the big picture. At least he's not disappointed. Even that relatively simple emotion is too big a task at the moment. Compared to Chris, the dwarf feels amazing. It won't last. He's just turned on. People romanticize these kinds of moments. I certainly have. But this is just an incomprehensible, private, interpersonal trip, i.e., something whose meaning is inseparable from the minute particularities of two strangers' chemistry.

Sue hit the gas. Maybe two seconds later, the slowly enlarging headlights grew a third one. It had vibrant, crusty edges and a cold, purplish center.

"Shit." Pam shut her eyes, prayed to the effect that if she wasn't arrested she'd . . . Jesus Christ, *anything.*

Radio: It was crushed to bits / And it looked like you and me.

"Be cool." Sue turned down the radio, pulled the car over. "Here's our story. We're dykes. We thought this was a great place to snuggle."

†

Smear's remaining three quarters are standing waist deep in the
Bel Age hotel's rooftop pool. Those were MTV's orders. It's meant
to make them look Beatles-esque, probably. Stupid Americans. Up
on the deck, some guy's running around with a camera. On the
diving board, some over-made-up but not unattractive bikini-clad
woman clicks on a directional mike. "How's the tour going?" she
wonders aloud. She points it at Smear. "As well as could be expected," says Damon. Neither he, guitarist Graham, nor Dave the
drummer are thinking a thing about Alex's absence. He always
pulls shit. "Where's your bassist?" she asks. She points the mike.
"That's him," Damon says, indicating a dead potted palm on the
pool deck. British humor. "What's the matter?" she wonders. "Can't
he swim?" American humor. Smear's members roll their eyes charm-
ingly. MTV loves it. It's so . . . so Beatles-y or something. "Great!
Thanks, lads." Cut.

      Mason tossed me his camera. "Can you do me a favor?" he
said. Then he dove face first into Alex's ass.
      "I fucking hate you," I say half-jokingly, and snap off a photo.
"I expect a full report later."
      Mason raised up and frowned at me. "Wait a second." Snap.
"You didn't even rim him, did you?" Snap. "What has that Luke
weirdo done to you, Dennis?" Snap. "And quit wasting the film."
      "Fuck off." I aim the camera at Alex's face. Snap.

Before I met Luke and reassessed my morality, my favorite image
on earth was a picture I'd found in an old German textbook on
violent death. It showed a very young boy who'd been axed in the
head by his father. Death had either freeze-framed the look on
his face or molded him a new one. He looked astonished. Like
he couldn't believe his life was already over. Point is, Alex just

brought him back. Actually, I used to see that boy's face every time Chris nodded out. I even thought about him watching Luke and Scott space out on acid. I wonder where they were. I wonder if their weirdly similiar expressions meant anything. I wonder if I've been there myself. Is the experience as indescribable as an acid trip? Or is what they felt so obvious that, to quote my mom, were it a snake, it would have already bitten me?

The dwarf fucked Chris's ass with the knife. "What are you hiding in here?" he said. The point had just bumped into something.

Chris's ass: kkyphtsllmb . . .

"Nothing," Chris said. Or maybe he just thought it. It might not have made it as far as a word.

The dwarf buried one hand inside Chris, felt around, and returned to the world with . . . well, a handful of gore to be blunt. But there was something peculiar inside it.

Scott has abandoned the "comic strip"—for tonight, anyway. Its style is too slavishy true to the Japanese model. Its mechanisms are far too reductive to signify . . . what? He doesn't even know what he wants it to do. He just has these conflicting emotions re Luke, that's all. And art's where he works out his shit. But it can only do so much, at least when so much of that shit is circumscribed by denial. So he files the finished pages and walks to his bedroom. It's the one uncomplicated place in his life. It's like the last oxygenated compartment in a sunken submarine. Once he has shut the door, stripped, and slid under the covers, there's nothing between Luke and him. Or maybe there's everything between them and nothing inside them.

Officer King had a receding blond crew cut. "We stopped you," he told Sue, "because we observed some suspicious behavior."

"Here." Sue handed over her license, registration. "Look, we're lesbians, okay? We were feeling romantic. We had a little spat, but it's cool now."

Officer Sullivan walked through the vacant lot, pointing a flashlight at everything that wasn't perfectly flat. Weed . . . McDonald's bag . . . cardboard box . . . "Oh, *shit*."

About Robert and Tracy. They used to be promising writers. Occasionally they'd show me their work, and I'd offer encouragement. Anyway, they developed this father fixation on me, as best I can tell. That happens a lot. I seem to encourage that behavior in people unconsciously. But once they got addicted to dope, they quit writing. We drifted apart. When I met Luke and became so devoted to him, they got paranoid and jealous. I used to hear all this shit secondhand. To make a long story short, they tried to get Luke on heroin, basically to hurt me. They said as much to Scott, who passed along the word. Luckily Luke was too scared to shoot up. But when I heard what they'd done, I chopped them out of my life. And now I've removed them from Luke's—in this novel, at least.

"I should go," I say. The roll's shot. Not to mention that the acid is finally dead or, at the very least, stagnant. I'm literally falling asleep.

Smear: Run, run, run, run, run, run, run, run . . .

Maybe it's just my mental haze, but I'd swear there's a smidgen more presence in Alex's face than there was a few minutes ago. "I hate to tell you this," I whisper. "But I think he's reviving."

Mason cranes his neck. "Hm, you're right." But he was certain I wasn't.

As soon as I left, Mason did what he'd thought about doing for hours. Actually, were that truly the case, Mason would have lobot-

omized Alex, or at least given it the old college try, à la Jeffrey
Dahmer. Instead, he fucked Alex harder than he'd fucked anyone
in his life. The physical effect was sublime, but it wasn't enough.
He wanted Alex to stay. Like, until they got old. Mason would
have settled for a zombie, if need be. That's how cute the boy was.
I can sort of relate. Maybe that's why we're still friends, despite
our incompatible morals. Difference is, I want to earn someone's
loyalty. I want to love someone so selflessly that he would never
even think about going away. I suppose that's what most people
want. In fact, that's probably why we don't kill one another all
the time. Everyone's just a little too lonely to risk it.

The dwarf turned on a faucet. He held the gore under the
spray. The sink purpled. "What the . . . ?"
It was just a big, petrified turd, glazed a yellowy white by a
hundred men's undisturbed come. But the dwarf didn't know anything about junkies and/or their little physical problems so . . .
Chris was this impossibly motionless humanesque form with
an astonished expression.
"Are you alive?" asked the dwarf. Maybe Chris's eyes altered
very slightly, or not. "Well, if you are, what the hell is this?"

Scott's having sex with a simplified Luke—in his dreams, anyway.
Their sex consists of Scott's hard-on, his blurry right hand, and
some chemical or other in his body. And his imagination, of course.
Scott's mental image of Luke is almost unrecognizable. On the
surface, sure, yeah, that's basically Luke. Activity-wise, though,
he might as well be some bimboesque slut. Granted, I don't know
how Luke acts in bed. But I'm positive this isn't it. Luke's too deep,
tense, reserved. Scott's spent too much time watching porn videos. Luke can't be reduced to the facts of his physical makeup. He's
too avant-garde, multilayered. That's why Scott's crazed ravish-

ing of the Luke look-alike doesn't bother me. He's not even
close.

"You're awake," Mason said. He was over at his work table,
pretending to glue something down. It was a small totem pole of
Goof heads for the record.

"I s'pose," Alex says blearily. He sits up. That's when he
knows something's wrong. His ass feels too . . . there. Normally,
it's just unassumedly doing its job. "Can you tell me the time?"

Sebadoh: It's not my job to undo / the dying prophecy of you.

"Almost five," Mason said. "I tried . . . to wake you up . . . a
few hours ago . . . but . . ."

The rest of Smear, plus their ex-skinhead roadie Gargantuan,
are watching *Little Women* on Showtime. At the moment, Amy
(Samantha Mathis) is pooh-poohing a marriage proposal from Laurie
(Christian Bale). "This bloke's a really good actor," says Graham
absentmindedly. "Mm," says Damon. "Wasn't he Alex's school-
mate?" asks Dave. At that very moment, a door in the real world
swings open. "What did you say about me?" says Alex, stumbling
inside. "Hey, mate. You look . . . beat," says Damon. "I don't want to
talk about it," says Alex. He flops onto a bed. Being English, Smear's
members maintain an innate, deep respect for emotional repression,
even between closest friends. But being English, they also absolutely
adore watching people get weepy in films. Alex registers the TV.
"Christian," he says. "You knew him," says Dave. "He's a friend of a
friend," says Alex. Then they space gratefully on the screen.

The dwarf made a deep, roughly circular incision around
Chris's ass crack. Then he dug in his hand, yanked, yanked, and
the cheeks lifted up like a soft manhole cover.

Chris: kkgghymddhj . . .

Blinking wildly, the dwarf studied Chris's op art–like, purplish-red, pasta-esque insides. He was looking for . . . something, anything. He didn't know. Some clue, some sign.

When I got home, the incense stink was so fierce that I guessed Luke had woken up while I was gone. But the stuff clings, that's all. Thank God, because I was in no state to talk. Ever since Mason's I'd felt sort of pissed off at him, at myself, at the world . . . I wasn't totally sure. Anger's the most foreign feeling to me. When I get angry, I tend to isolate, drink very heavily, lie around, stare, and play strange mental games like . . . Devise the perfect suicide. For the record, I've settled on: Tell friends you're going to Europe, hike into some forest, dig a grave, lie down in it, put a gun in your mouth, and blow your brains out, simultaneously triggering a small avalanche that will fill in the grave.

"Damon," says Alex. Graham and Dave have gone back to their rooms. "Something rather . . . untoward has happened." Then he tells his favorite bandmate what he's been imagining.

"Bloody hell!" Damon slugs Gargantuan from his nap, then reiterates Alex's tale with a lot less complexity.

"I'll fookin' *kill* the blagger," yells Gargantuan. He grabs Alex's arm. "Where does he live? Tell me!"

As a pseudo-sophisticate, Alex deplores violence. But being sweet, he's so touched by their concern that— "Here," he says, and reaches into his pocket. "The fellow gave me his card."

So maybe it wasn't shit after all. Maybe it was some sort of magical, mystical object that God or whoever had hidden in Chris's clogged bowels, thinking no one would bother to search there.

That might explain why the dwarf felt so trippy. See, unless his brain was more damaged than doctors let on, that wasn't a densely packed swirl of intestines, bones, organs, and so on, it was a whole, unique, miniaturized world complete with roads, towns, mountains, lakes, national parks. It was so beautiful. And best of all, the dwarf felt huge and all-powerful by comparison. Not that he knew what to do with his new superpowers. Other than to completely destroy what he'd been given to play with, of course.

There's a fax drooping out of my answering machine. So I rip it free, and flop into an armchair.

Fax: Dear Dennis, You asked after Vincent "Sniffles" Cochrane. He's not doing well, and is unable to answer your fax personally at this time . . .

Blur: All you ever do is fade away / All you ever do is fade away.

Fax: . . . If you care to visit him, please call ahead. He has his good days and bad days, but we encourage . . .

Pam and Sue are locked into the back of a squad car. Is this fair? It's an interesting question—to me, anyway. Goof died of natural causes. No paramedic in the world could have brought him back to life sans enormous brain damage. The way Pam and Sue had it planned, Goof's body would have been found, identified. Phoning the cops would have meant a lengthy jail term for Pam and the end of her kiddie porn venture. Granted, the exploitation of children is evil. No question. I agree. That's a very good general rule. But people's lives aren't just indistinguishable examples of some overriding, concrete, correct way of thinking. And there's a way in which Pam's work was noble. Or maybe I'm saying that it's been important to me. But then, I'm sick.

†

"Mason," I tell his phone machine. "Pick the fuck up." When he does, I calm down very slightly. I'm such a wuss. "Is the Smear guy still there?"

There's a sniff. "No, we parted ways, oh, an hour ago."

Blur: I feel so unnecessary / We don't think so, you seem star-shaped.

"Look, we need to talk about what we just did, because I've been thinking about it, and—"

"If you wish." Mason's voice had this twist. "But can you hold on a second? There's someone at my door."

Mason's away from the phone for . . . well, just a couple of minutes, I guess. But it feels like forever. I can hear Sebadoh in the background. "Brand New Love," I think. Plus some yells and commotion, presumably from the street. I'm too pissed off to wait, frankly. So after saying his name several times, I hang up on the fucker. God, I'm fried, which is nice considering how bad I'd be feeling if I had a functional brain. One of the beautiful things about LSD's decomposition is how it eventually strands users' minds at a point—I'm talking post-hallucination, post-disorientation, post-speediness—where you're sort of like . . . I don't know, a TV set with its picture blown out. You can talk, but it doesn't add up. You're useless, and you might as well turn yourself off. I'm there.

When I get to the bed, Luke's a log. At some point he took off his shirt, and the sheets have settled down in a bunch at his waist.

Luke: zzhbtyllkspp . . .

Good thing I'm pooped, because I've never seen anything more beautiful in my life than his back. God, I sound so ridiculous.

"Luke," I say softly. My voice is too quiet to wake him. That's okay. It's for the best. I don't know what I was thinking.

Mason's sprawled in his doorway. Gargantuan's kicking the shit out of him. Scott just came. Pam and Sue are filed away inside freezing cold cells. You can basically forget them. Goof's right where he was, just extremely flashlit and surrounded by cops. Smear's getting drunk. The dwarf is carving a corpse into disposable bits. It used to be Chris. Luke's asleep. I'm asleep to his immediate right, or I will be any second.

Star-Shaped

As I recall, I woke around noon, checked the bed, realized Luke was already up, then got dressed in a hurry and hit the kitchen. Acid hangovers are nice; I'd forgotten. You feel robotic and spacy, or I did. I put on some coffee, brushed my teeth, shaved, then filled my favorite cup, which changes color according to the temperature of its contents, and carried it into the living room. Luke was sitting on the couch, a spiral notebook in his lap, writing something in faint pencil.

"I was just about to leave you a note," he said.

"Yeah, sorry." I flopped down in my armchair.

He shut the notebook. "I'm going back to my place, pack up, spend the night there, then bring my things over tomorrow, if that seems okay."

"Sure."

"So . . ." Luke smiled nonchalantly. It didn't quite work. His face is a horrible hiding place. "When I live here, where am I going to sleep?"

"You can have the office," I said.

He looked uncertain.

"I'll move the desk into my bedroom."

"Oh, cool," he said. But he still looked uncertain.

"What?" I sipped some more coffee. The cup was red.

He slid the notebook into his backpack. "I just think we should talk."

"Sure. But can you wait a few minutes? I'm sort of senile until I've had two cups of coffee."

Luke zipped the backpack. "I'll give you a call later, then," he said, and hooked the strap over his shoulder. "Because I kind of have to go."

"Okay, but what is it?"

"Nothing bad." He grinned goofily and shot to his feet, un-folding and seeming to lift very slightly off the floor for a second or two like a string puppet. "I'll leave these here. You should play them." He indicated a heap of cassettes on the arm of the couch. Then he made an abrupt, roughly star-shaped tour of the room, as if he'd misplaced his car keys, although I could see them in his hand.

"Will do."

Luke's tour landed him at the door of my office. It was ajar, but he pushed it wide open. I guess I'd left on the light.

"It's kind of small," I said.

"No, it's perfect. So who are those guys on your bulletin board?"

"People who interest me." I sipped a little coffee. The cup was orangey.

"They all look alike."

"Yeah, I know."

He disappeared into the room. "They look like me," said his voice.

"That's true."

"What interests you about them?" I heard his T-shirt brush over my can of pens and pencils, so he might have been leaning in close to the pictures.

"I don't know."

"They're cute," said his voice. I couldn't tell if he was kidding.

"Yeah."

Luke reappeared in the doorway. "Is that why they interest you?" He seemed to be studying me.

"Partly." I sipped a little coffee. The cup was orange.

"So . . . I'll call you later," he said.

When the door shut, I made a decision. It was very complicated, and I wouldn't know how to describe it. It might have resembled the kinds of decisions guys make just before they get married or join the army or turn themselves in to the cops or begin to kick drugs. I mean, when they give themselves one stretch of time to go totally wild for the very last time. Then I remembered the fax from the AIDS hospice, walked into my office, and called the number on the letterhead. I told some guy that I'd come visit Sniffles late that afternoon, hung up, checked my date book, confirmed Drew's arrival time, then took a quick, unremarkable shower.

The doorbell rang. I was in the kitchen, drinking a glass of V8. Its opaqueness was weirding me out, I don't know why. It just seemed wrong. I poured the remaining juice into the sink, washed out the glass, strolled into the living room, and aligned my right eye with the spy hole. Drew was wearing a giant white R.E.M. T-shirt, black denim cutoffs, and pale green Nikes. He had a large, folksy head, blue eyes, a precious nose, big lips and ears, and an unkempt mod haircut with weirdly long bangs. His arms were skinny and tanned.

His legs were chubby and almost fluorescent. A skateboard was wedged into one of his armpits. To keep it aloft, he'd had to thrust out a leg, which might explain why I thought he looked slutty. He was holding a large gift-wrapped box. Every second or two he would look down and check himself out in its gold Mylar paper.

I opened the door very fast. It just seemed like a plan.

Drew's head snapped up. First he looked shocked, then he tried to adopt a "who cares?" attitude, but a crooked smile ruined the effect he was going for, I guess, and he said, "Fuck."

"So, yeah."

He came inside and walked into the living room. "Oh, this guy," he said. He went straight to Scott's drawing.

"Can I get you something to drink?"

"I probably should, huh?" He squinted at the drawing. "What does this mean?"

I thought for a second. "It's art."

"My dad says art isn't about anything until someone buys it. Then it's about the person who owns it."

Whatever. "So what do you want to drink?"

"Do you have any tequila?"

"I think so."

"Cool." Drew leaned in close, studying some detail or other of the drawing. Then he either grew bored or feigned boredom, tore his eyes from the picture, and scanned the living room. He chose the couch, sat roughly in the middle, dropped the skateboard onto the floor and gave it a kick through the room, then set the gift-wrapped box down on the coffee table. I guess he saw me studying it. "It's a present for you," he said. "I think you're gonna like it."

I walked into the kitchen, got the bottle of Cuervo Gold out of the cupboard, filled a tumbler, then dropped in some ice cubes. Somewhere along the way I decided the box held a dildo. It just seemed to make sense, and I liked the idea. When I returned with the drink I had a scary, unmistakable hard-on. It caused this weird effect in Drew's eyes, maybe fear, maybe lust. Whatever the mood, it created a slight dissonance in his childish appearance. Admittedly, I was grasping for straws. I sat to his right. I mean, so close that my hip skidded down the side of his body. Then I handed him the drink, rested my huge, chilly hand on his warm, bony knee, and thought, Okay, I get it. I mean, why people fuck guys half their size, weight, maturity, et cetera. It had something to do with a general tenderness toward the young, and something to do with my hangover, and something to do with the chubbiness of his legs. That's pretty much all I can say about that.

"Whoa," Drew said, looking at the glass. But I think he meant my hard-on. He took a ludicrously gigantic swallow.

"Tough guy."

Drew's eyes teared. "So much"—cough—"shit, so much for your thing on the phone . . . about"—cough—"about not wanting to . . . fuck me, liar."

"This doesn't mean I'm going to fuck you. It just means you're cute, which you already know."

"You think I'm cute." His voice was all strangled.

"Fuck you. You know I do." To prove my point, I eased several fingertips inside the leg of his cutoffs.

He was struggling not to look down. "As cute as that guy you like in Smear?"

"Pretty damn close," I said, and scooched in my fingers another few inches. The denim was bunched in two tight, impassable folds along the borderline of his crotch, but I could feel the sticky warmth of his scrunched dick and balls maybe an inch farther on.

"As cute as that guy you really like? What's his name? Lou?"

"Luke. No."

Drew looked confused. "Wait. He's that guy I saw you with at that art opening once, right? He's not that cute at all."

"Point is, I'm not going to fuck you."

"What's your problem?" Drew whined. He frowned down at my hand. "I mean, come on."

"You know what the problem is. You're fourteen."

"I'm cool about it."

"I know."

"And I'm big for my age."

"Yeah, but—"

"*It's no big deal.*" Drew seemed exasperated. He flopped back onto the cushions and cradled his head in his hands. The change in position inflated the front of his cutoffs, accidentally clearing my route to his crotch. So before they resettled, I reached in and felt him up, just out of curiosity. His dick was finger-size, hard, weirdly dry, and very hot at the tip, like a lit cigarette.

"It is to me," I said.

Drew's eyes shut. "But . . . we talked about this on the phone, and . . . oh, my God, that feels cool . . . and you told me you had these . . . sick fantasies. And how you collected that cute guy's pubic hairs and all that. And I'm completely cool about anything weird."

"Listen, you have no idea," I said. Touching his dick had made everything too realistic or something.

Drew's eyes opened a fraction. "I need to take a leak," he said.

"Sorry."

Phew. "It's over there." I extracted my fingers. As they came free, I got a tentative whiff of his crotch. Luckily, it smelled pissy.

"Show me," Drew said. He looked sly. But then he always looked sly. The kid's face was just permanently sly, like a rock is permanently a random pattern wrapped around a roughly spherical form.

†

Drew faced the toilet, unzipped his cutoffs, reached down inside, and pulled out his hard-on. He tried to aim, but the little thing was too stiff, so he bent his knees slightly, stuck out his ass, and almost managed to line up his dick with the bowl. Then he shot a weak, jittery arc of piss, most of which ended up on the floor. Mason had been insisting that as delectable as Drew's ass looked on tape, it wasn't in fact photogenic at all, and I'd thought, Yeah, whatever. But thanks to Drew's dumb, inadvertently lewd-looking stance, his ass had materialized in the jeans—crack, indentations, and all, albeit slightly stylized by the denim. As I studied the results, my imagination got sort of enmeshed in the perfection of it all, not unlike when I'd first seen *Star Wars* and thought, Yeah, if I saw that Death Star thing floating in space, I'd turn bad in a second.

"Okay, you win," I said.

Drew looked back at me, one eye scrunched, confused, or wanting me to think he was confused.

"I changed my mind," I said

Drew's cutoffs were so filthy their black had an asphaltesque glimmer, especially the seat, which looked like a silk-screened image of the universe and radiated this sweet, earthy, hashish-like stink. He was lying in front of my TV, awaiting the show. I was kneeling to his immediate left, bent way over, feeling his ass through the denim. At one point I paused, grabbed the videotape, and fed my VCR. I'd labeled the tape MASON DREW THIS, so that no one going through my collection of videos would ever be tempted to play it, no matter how bored they were. Then I grabbed the remote with one hand and recaptured Drew's ass with the other. It had two distinct modes. Either it was doughy and flat, a tide pool crudely framed by his hipbones, or it was as hard as a helmet and practically pinged when I touched it. It kept shifting back and forth, hard, soft, hard, soft, according to some game in Drew's mind.

"Punch it," Drew said. "The tape, not my ass, heh heh."

I aimed the remote and pushed PLAY.

On TV, Drew was alone, sprawled on Mason's bed, jerking off with one hand and caressing his chest with the other. Mason's voice said, "I can't seem to find it." Then he entered the picture, sat down on the bed, squinted into the lens, i.e., at us, and said, "I'm going to leave on the lights." Then Drew said, "Oh, my God, really?" Then Mason, still looking at us, said, "You deserve it," turned sideways, batted Drew's hand away from the dick, and replaced it with his own.

"I love when my hair looks like that," Drew said.

"So what were you thinking?" I wondered.

"What do you mean?"

"Then," I said. "While he was jerking you off."

"I don't know. I was probably hoping my hair looked okay. I'm really cute, aren't I?"

"Well, duh."

On TV, Mason kept jerking Drew off. He said, "I'm imagining you're Chris Gentry from Menswear, so if I call you Chris, or say something that sounds incongruous, don't worry." Then Drew raised himself up on his elbows and said, "What is Menswear? Everybody keeps saying I look like somebody in Menswear." Then Mason said, "They're a cute, flash, disposable British pop band. Can you pretend you're asleep?" Then Drew said, "Whatever, sure," and did a kooky pratfall. Then his unconscious body said, "Are they any good?" Then Mason stood up, walked to the head of the bed, and blocked our view of Drew's face with his ass. Then his ass started jiggling, and there were the faint squishy sounds of a mouth being fucked. Then Mason said, "They're all right."

"This part's boring," Drew said. "How long does this last?"

"Longer than it should."

"So I'd look cute if I was dead, hunh?" Drew looked back at me—or, should I say, he tried to, because his neck wasn't all that flexible, so I doubt he saw much.

"Maybe for ten minutes."

Drew looked hurt. "What do you mean?"

"Well, you'd stiffen up."

Drew thought about that. "I could still look cute, couldn't I? One time my dad took a picture of me all crashed out and I thought I looked hot." He turned to the screen. "This is taking forever."

"Did you ever see that picture of River Phoenix in his coffin?"

"No, unh-unh."

I got up, walked into my office, opened a drawer in the file cabinet, raised the River Phoenix file an inch higher than the rest, flipped through the dozens of stills, tear sheets, and magazine articles until I found a yellowed clipping I'd ripped from the *National Enquirer*, then closed the drawer and returned to the living room.

"Can I fastforward through this?" he asked.

"It's almost over. Here, look."

Drew turned just enough to snatch the clipping, then flattened it out on the rug. "Wow."

"Yeah, well, that's death."

"Oh, my God, you mean I'd look like that? No way. It's because he did heroin."

In the picture, River Phoenix, whose cultist parents were spiritually opposed to beautifying the dead, was visibly rotting away.

"Hopefully you'll be so old when you die that it won't be that big of a shift." That felt evil.

On TV, Mason's ass cheeks stopped jiggling. He backed toward the camera. "Give me a second," he said. "Don't move." Then he walked out of the picture. Then a very flushed, screwy-eyed, come-splattered Drew said, "That was cool," and licked some sperm off his lips. Then Mason's voice said, "You could say that." Then Drew swallowed the sperm and said, "It must have been cool to see your dick in my mouth." Then Mason's voice said, "How so?" Then Drew, looking a little confused, said, "You know, because I'm cute," and laughed nervously. Then Mason's voice said, "What a curious statement." Then Drew, looking more confused, said, "What do you mean?" Then Mason's voice said, "Well, that you can be so objective." Then Drew, who didn't seem to understand what Mason meant, said, "Oh, sorry." Then Mason's voice said, "No need to apologize."

Drew frowned at the screen. "My hair's a mess," he said. "It should always be hanging in my eyes, like it is now." He turned slightly to show me.

"Why?" The difference seemed subtle. I'd just reached beneath Drew's waist, found the snap on his jeans, popped it, found the little zipper tab and was dragging it all the way down.

"Because I have a weird forehead." He turned and grinned at me. "What are you doing?"

"How is it weird?" I extracted my hands, then gripped the seat of his cutoffs and worked them down to his knees. The long, flimsy tail of his T-shirt was still in my way, but I lifted it up ceremoniously. His ass was doing its helmet thing, and yeah, okay, it was technically perfect, and yeah, okay, when I touched it I felt kind of faint.

"I don't know," Drew said. "It just is." He reached back and squeezed his ass, maybe checking for lint, maybe to turn himself on. He handled each cheek, dug a fingertip into his ass crack, itched, itched, then brought that finger up to his nose and took a sniff.

"What's the verdict?" I asked.

Drew looked horrified. "What? Oh, heh heh, I smell kind of cool. Check it out." And he held out the finger. Luckily, it smelled gross.

My plan was to get Drew's ass out in the open, then let whatever happened happen. I'd figured its beauty would dictate my behavior, i.e., what I said before about the Death Star. But in person the ass was a little too cutesy or something. Maybe if I'd been a kid I could have decoded whatever was sleazy and/or delicious about it, but I wasn't, of course, so it was more like I'd just been given a toy that I was slightly too old for. Then I got an idea.

On TV, Drew was fingering his bangs into place. In life, he was cringing and shielding his eyes from the sight of his half-exposed forehead.

"You're in the clear," I said. I tried to pry his little ass cheeks apart with my thumbs, but the things might as well have been carved out of one piece of wood. "Relax your ass, okay?"

Drew checked the screen. "Yeah, but my hair can be *so much better.*"

"Relax your ass." I sounded angrier than I felt.

"What? Oh, right." It collapsed.

On TV, Mason was back in the picture. He set a jar of lubricant on the night table and unscrewed its lid, then joined Drew on the bed. Then Drew eyeballed the lube and said, "Cool." Then Mason said, "Glad you think so," and pursed his lips like he does when he's thinking. Then Drew looked at Mason's lips and said, "What?" Then Mason said, "You know how in calisthenics there's this one exercise where you pretend like you're riding a bike in the air?" Then Drew said, "Sure." Then Mason said, "Do that now, only don't pump your legs." Then Drew said, "Cool," positioned himself, and said, "What do I do with my legs?" Then Mason took one of Drew's ankles in each hand, parted his legs, and said, "Keep them like that." Then Drew scrunched up his face and tried very, very hard to stabilize his lower body. Then Mason said, "Perfect," and buried his tongue in Drew's asshole.

"Wouldn't it be cool if you could sleep with yourself?" Drew asked.

"Maybe in your case."

"Sometimes when I jerk off, I look in a mirror. Is that weird?"

"What? Oh, not in your case." I was trying to think.

I got this idea of how to flush the innocence from Drew's body. I mean, so I could think about fucking or eating him out or whatever. It involved digging my thumbs into his ass crack, prying it open, then smearing the cheeks to their respective sides of Drew's body and securing them there with my fists. It was harder to do than it sounds. Things kept escaping. When every muscle and fat globule was in place, and the ass cheeks were razed, there was nothing to see but a smallish, misshapen plateau with a crude, pink, indented triangular splotch in the center.

"What are you doing?" Drew asked. He tried to look back, and I guess he saw something, however vague, because his eyes bugged. "Wow, that's intense. Is it still sexy? Because I can't tell."

I thought for a second. "In the context of your body, yeah."

"Cool." He turned and checked the TV. "Okay, I know why Mason did this, heh heh." He squinted. "I have a weird look on my face. What does it look like I'm thinking?"

"You tell me," I said.

On TV, Mason was dabbing the lube onto Drew's asshole. Then he wiped off his gooey fingertips on the bed, aimed his dick, pressed its head to Drew's asshole, and shoved. Then Drew sucked in a gigantic breath and said, "Shit." Then Mason said, "Please don't make noise." Then Drew pounded the bed with his fists and said, "Sorry, I'm sorry, I just thought . . ." but he couldn't continue. Then Mason pulled his dick all the way out of Drew's ass, paused, re-aimed, shoved it all the way in, and said, "What?" Then Drew breathed noisily a few times and said, "That you should always wear a condom." Then Mason said, "No, that's not true." Then Drew opened his mouth very wide, closed it, sort of shrieked, and said, "Oh."

"Just that it was cool, I guess," Drew said. He was studying himself. "Do you think my voice is weird? Because sometimes I think it's kind of . . . nosy. Or what do you call it?"

"Nasal. Come on, you must have been thinking more than that."

"What do you mean?"

"I mean, you have emotions. You're not stupid."

"Really? You think so?"

I was suddenly so sick of giving him compliments. "Yeah. Look, shut up for a minute." I freed his ass, and it bounced back.

"Why?" He turned and glanced worriedly at his ass, then at me.

"So I can pretend you're that Menswear guy."

"Him again," Drew said sort of huffily.

Then I got an idea.

I crossed my legs, patted one of my knees, and said, "Here." Drew raised himself up, like he was beginning a push-up. I slid my thighs underneath him. He collapsed, bent and unbent his legs until he was comfortable, then fixed his eyes on the screen. I spanked Drew for several minutes, and he laughed hysterically, and his ass got really smudgy and stupid. It fascinated me, sort of like that heat-sensitive coffee cup fascinates me, but I wasn't exactly turned on. So after a while I gave up and thought, Maybe if he was unconscious. It sounds like a huge mental leap, but actually it was just the next obvious idea in line. About then the video ended, conveniently enough.

"Close your eyes," I said. "Don't move."

I eased out from under him, walked to my bookcase, and removed *The New Murderer's Handbook,* by Richard K. Krousher. I found the chapter on head injuries, then located the specific paragraph that described how you could hit someone on one particular part of the head, knock him unconscious, and cause permanent motor dysfunction without actually killing him. I replaced the book, walked to where the skateboard had rolled, picked it up, found a good place for it in my hands, then walked back to Drew and realized pretty quickly that it was going to be too hard to aim when his head was that close to the floor.

"I'm going to help you up," I said, and grabbed ahold of his forearm. "But don't open your eyes or you'll ruin it."

"This is really cool," Drew said as I hauled him to his knees. "I mean, like, 'What's he going to do?'"

Drew's chest was splotchy and pink—from the carpet, I guess —and he had a pointy hard-on, and his ass looked like a big vegetable, and—with his eyes shut, at least—his resemblance to Menswear's Chris Gentry was kind of unnerving. "Open your eyes," I said.

The first thing he saw was the skateboard. "Oh, cool," he said.

"What do you want to be when you grow up?"

He looked bemused. "That's funny."

"I'm serious."

"I don't know. Something to do with art."

"You want to be an artist?"

"Sure."

"What do you want to express as an artist?"

"Oh, my God, seriously?" He closed his eyes, rumpled his face, made a few swishy noises with his mouth, then smiled and re-opened his eyes. "The void at the center of everything."

I guess I looked shocked.

"I'm kidding. No, my dad said that once about some painting he owns. I don't want to be an artist. Artists are too weird. I wouldn't mind if some artist fell in love with me and did nothing but make art about me and we got really famous and rich. That would be kind of cool."

"That's sort of more what I thought you'd say."

"Yeah?" he asked. He looked at the skateboard. "So what's that for?"

"I'm going to knock you unconscious," I said.

He laughed. "How?"

"I'm going to hit you on the head with it."

"Oh, sure," he said.

"You won't die. It'll just make you sort of a zombie."

"Oh, right," he said sarcastically.

I assumed this position I vaguely remembered from gym class or somewhere, legs spread, all my weight on the right. I pretended the board was a bat and raised it over my shoulder. Then I thought about nailing Drew's head. I imagined the staticky pop as it cracked. I saw him collapse. I saw myself pounce. I saw myself chew, lick, fuck, fist-fuck, claw, strangle, and whittle away until he was just a big oily red stain on my floor. It gave me a frightening hard-on. But maybe because Drew didn't think I could do such a thing, or maybe because I'm just not very evil, I couldn't go through with it. Or I didn't in this case. It was a simple decision, seconds long, pain free, but I wouldn't know how to describe how I made it. Point is, it felt like no big deal whatsoever, although it was easily the most significant decision I'd ever made. Anyway, I lowered the skateboard. "Kidding," I said.

"Duh." Drew sat back on his calves. He stretched, cracked his neck. His whole body emitted these soft little pops.

Then I got an idea.

I strolled into my office and dialed Mason's number. He always screened calls, but I was sure he'd pick up if I used a particular tone of voice. It was our code for when one of us had an idea whose implementation required the services of a mock evil twin. I wouldn't know how to describe it. Anyway, it worked.

"Yeah, hi," he said. "Did you hear what happened to me? Oh, right, we were on the phone."

"Scott told me some guy beat you up."

"Smear's roadie," Mason said.

"You okay?"

"No, but it was worth it."

"So look," I said. "Drew's here and there's a remote chance I'm going to kill him. You want to come over and film it?"

Mason snickered, I think. "Sure. This is a switch."

"You know me," I said, and hung up.

I returned to the living room. Drew was lying facedown on the rug. I'd covered his mouth with electrical tape, blindfolded him with the R.E.M. T-shirt, and tied his wrists with a sock. When I approached, the floor creaked, and he tried to say something, but thanks to the tape, his conversational skills had been reduced to an appreciative "mm." It was nice.

"Mason's coming over to film us," I said. "That's cool, right?"

"Mm."

"Just play along with whatever I say, okay? I'm going to tell him I've knocked you unconscious."

I think Drew laughed, but it sounded like "Mm mm mm mm," so as far as I knew, he could have been pleading with me to untie him.

I let Mason in. When I saw the damage Smear's roadie had done to his face, I had this bizarre déjà vu. You know, as though he had walked through the door in a previous life. Strange. Then the déjà vu cross-faded into an LSD flashback, I guess. I was back in the kitchen eyeballing that glass of V8, and the doorbell was ringing. Then I was back in Mason's presence again. I have no idea what it means. Anyway, it only lasted a second or two, after which we exchanged our hellos. Then he walked into the living room, saw Drew tied up, grabbed his videocam, put it up to his eye, and said, "Well, I'm impressed."

"Yeah, thanks," I said.

"What's wrong with him?" The damage to Mason's face had made him seem more implacable than ever.

"I hit him on the head," I said. "With that skateboard."

Mason aimed at the skateboard. "You're not really going to kill him."

"I don't know."

"But I thought you'd gone raver."

"I need to do this to put me over the hump," I said. "Why, what's your justification?"

"Oh, I have no problem with it." Mason panned around the room. When his lens hit the couch, he zoomed in. "What's that?"

We spent the next maybe twenty, twenty-five minutes opening Drew's little gift. I'd told Drew about my collection of Paul souvenirs during one of our phone conversations, and I guess it had made an impression. What he'd given to me was a kind of Drew Baldwin

Museum-ette. There were three small pill bottles. One held a half dozen nail clippings. One held a brown pubic hair. One held a brownish red flake. That bottle's label read NOSEBLEED. There was a bulging envelope on which Drew had scrawled, I NEED THESE BACK. SORRY. It held a ragged deck of different-size photos. Most were Polaroids of Drew nude on a bed, hard and/or spreading his ass cheeks. He'd written stupid things on their backs like COME AND GET IT and WORSHIP ME. One showed a poorly lit, middle-age man who might or might not have been a local art dealer, Harry something or other. On its back Drew had scrawled, HE PAID ME TWO HUNDRED BUCKS FOR MY USED UNDERWEAR. CAN YOU BELIEVE IT?! There were old shots of Drew in his crib, at his third birthday party, at Disneyland, at the zoo, in a Witchiepoo Halloween costume. Deeper down in the box, we found three mayonnaise jars. One was half-filled with piss. One contained a small turd. One was opaque with vomit. The whole thing was just so unbelievably charming— to us, anyway. And I thought, I can't kill this kid. He's too . . . something.

"Do you think he's read Proust?" Mason was studying a shot of the very young Drew petting a llama. I'm not sure what he saw in there.

"Doubt it."

He handed me the photo. "The kid's brilliant. I had no idea."

"It's a really great gift." I started putting everything back in the box.

"Oh, it's incredible," Mason said, watching the stuff go away.

I paused on one of the new Polaroids. It was a close-up of Drew's ass. The shot had been overexposed and was just out of focus. "Didn't you say you've had cannibal fantasies?"

"Sure." He peeked over my shoulder.

"I'd eat this in a second."

"Absolutely."

I checked the real thing. Maybe it was the ropes, or Drew's goose bumps, or the lingering, post-spanking flush, but in person the ass looked more like something you'd actually eat than something you'd fantasize about eating. "How would one go about that?" I wondered.

"I don't know. Does your fireplace work?"

"Last I checked."

"We could cram him in there."

I guess our fantasy was too creepy for Drew. He blew his cover, said, "Mm mm mm," and started rocking around on the floor.

"Uh-oh," Mason said. He glanced at me.

I tried not to smirk, but I did.

Mason studied my smirk for a second. "You're hopeless," he said. Then he smirked too. So naturally I assumed he'd understood my charade. When he stood up and headed for Drew, I was sure he'd untie the poor kid. When he picked up the skateboard, it seemed like black humor. When he slammed the skateboard down on Drew's head, I was extremely surprised. "Like that?" he said, and looked over at me.

"I don't know," I said. I was sort of in shock. "Drew?"

The boy was incredibly still. I mean like a freeze-frame. Unless you've seen someone unconscious, it's hard to describe.

"For real," I said. "You have my permission to talk. Are you okay?"

Mason discarded the skateboard, crouched, and started fingering the back of Drew's head. "Was it supposed to indent?" he asked. "Because it didn't."

Mason was filming the unconscious Drew. We'd untied him. He'd been lying on his back for a while. Now he was facedown again. Mason's lens was skimming over the ass in this unbroken, sort of diagnostic caress. We were naked except for our T-shirts and socks. I was sitting cross-legged a few feet away from them, watching the shoot. "Can I ask you a favor?" Mason said.

"I guess." I'd gotten very depressed.

"It's huge."

"What?" I sounded more impatient than I felt.

"Can I finish him off?" Mason said.

"What, now?"

"Actually, I was thinking of taking him home."

In my decayed mental state, that seemed fine. I just wanted Drew to resonate again. In a hospital bed, at Mason's, dissolving in my stomach, charred in the fireplace, it didn't really matter. Or I felt like it didn't. Besides, Mason and I had this code, as I think I've explained, so I knew he wasn't going to kill Drew. Not really. Plus I had stuff to do. "Yeah, go ahead."

"You're a peach," he said. "So how do I keep him alive? Because I want to make some art with him first."

If I'd known, I would have told Mason.

"I'll figure something out," he continued. He switched off the videocam.

I checked my dick, which was so hard and itchy I felt like a teenager. Really, I had this distinct memory of lying in bed in my parents' house studying the first gay porn magazine I ever bought. It was called *Hard Up #3*, and it featured this skinny blond boy and this pockmarked older guy who was totally nuts about the skinny blond's ass. "I wonder what this is about?" I thwacked my dick.

"The kid's ass is Satan, I'm telling you." Mason got up, then grabbed his jeans off the floor and started putting them on. "I'll pull my car into the driveway."

I drove across town to the AIDS hospice. Once upon a time it had been your average everyday minimall, complete with a 7-Eleven where I'd occasionally bought beer. They'd painted the whole complex white, windows and all. The lobby was decorated with art—drawings, paintings, and framed photographs, most of which portrayed naked men stretching their arms toward the sun. When I reached the desk, there was a sign. It said that the art was created by patients, and that most of the works were for sale, proceeds benefiting the hospice. The artists' names were followed by parenthesized dates indicating the year they were born and, if they were dead, which most of them were, the year they died. I scanned the list. Sniffles was down near the bottom. Then I toured the show until I found his contribution, a Polaroid thumbtacked crookedly to the wall, showing him in his hospital bed. He'd scratched the words I GOT FUCKED into its surface. It wasn't bad at all. He still looked like Sniffles, the way a wilted flower looks like a flower. But his eyes had that empty, shocked glint that unifies the terminally ill and makes them look like dolls made in some Eastern Bloc country. About that time I heard a toilet flush, and a chunky blond clone wandered into the lobby. One of his fingers was wedged into a copy of *Stroke* magazine, and there was a definite, hard-on-shaped bump in the crotch of his jeans. He sat behind the desk, opened the magazine, laid it across his lap, and asked if he could help me with something.

"I called," I said. "About visiting Sniffles."

"Of course." He opened a drawer, reached in, removed a printed form, and placed it on the counter.

"Do you know him well?" I asked.

"Everyone knows everyone here."

"What do you think of him?"

He looked annoyed, then shut his eyes for a moment; when he reopened them he was serene—on the surface, at least. "You mean Vincent, the boy with the mohawk," he said.

"Yeah."

"He's in the terminal stages of AIDS, so there's not much to think."

"Well, thanks," I said. That sounded more sarcastic than I felt.

"I need to see some identification." The clone opened a drawer, reached in, removed a pen. "You said you're a friend," he added, and click-clicked the pen.

"Yeah." I reached for my wallet, then removed my license and handed it over.

The clone aligned the form and license, then started to copy my info. He'd barely gotten anywhere, maybe half to two thirds of the way through my name, when his forehead crumpled, his eyes grew staticky, and the pen hit the desktop. He leaned back in his chair and scowled at me. "Are you the writer?" he asked.

I just smiled at him.

"You wrote that article in *Spin* about Vincent."

"Yeah."

"Vincent's very proud of that article. Before he entered the terminal stages of AIDS, he used to make the staff read it to him every night. Personally, I thought your approach was exploitative in the extreme."

"I guess you had to be there," I said. Obviously, that was a joke. It just popped out. Sometimes I forget what a specialized world I've constructed around myself, full of people who listen for subtexts and tones within tones, and for whom I never need to pretend I have one clear emotion re anything.

He swept the form into his lap. It landed upside down on the *Stroke* magazine, which was spread to a double-page shot of some nude pumped-up guy with a handlebar mustache. "I'm going to decline your request."

"Why?" I guess I shot him a murderous glare. I didn't mean to. I was just tired and tense and maybe slightly appalled by his taste in men.

"That's why," he said. He pointed at my face.

I should have feigned shock, demanded my rights, and waltzed into the depths of the hospice. For whatever reason, I didn't. I just retrieved my driver's license, turned around, and left. On my way out I snatched Sniffles's Polaroid right off the wall. I mean, it wasn't as if the clone was going to phone the police. The thing only cost ten tax-deductible bucks. And unless you'd been physically into the artist before he got ravaged by AIDS, it wasn't worth anything—as an investment, I mean. When I got to the car, I shoved the Polaroid into my shirt pocket, then headed home, feeling extremely depressed but a little hungover and tired, which made the sensation okay. At one point I made a snap decision to drop by Mason's place unannounced, I don't know why. Maybe I wanted to save Drew. That's a pretty good guess, anyway. When I buzzed, there was a clatter of shoes down the stairs, then the door opened wide. Mason's face was in the monstrous early stages of healing. Deep down amid the bruises and scabs, he seemed sort of . . . I don't know, disappointed to see me?

"You look strange," he said.

"Yeah, I'm sure. Look, I want to see Drew."

His face hunted for something in mine. "You sort of can't," he said.

"Why?"

Mason scrunched up his lips and his eyes went unfocused. "He's dead."

That was way, way too perfect. "Bullshit."

"No, he is."

"How?"

"I was washing him off in the bathtub, and he accidentally drowned."

"I don't believe you."

"It's true." Mason shrugged.

"So let me see the body," I said.

Mason hunted my face again. "Listen, just let it go. I'll deal with it."

"You're so full of shit." I took a step in his direction, expecting him to clear out of my way, but he grabbed for the doorknob, which pissed me off.

"No, he's really dead." Then Mason cracked a little smile. "Okay, he's not dead. He regained consciousness and we're in love."

"He's not in love with you."

"Okay, but I'm in love with him, he's game, and I'm asking you as a friend to let me have him."

"You're not in love with him."

"Okay, I'm obsessed with him. What's the difference?"

I took another step. Mason grabbed again for the doorknob, then reconsidered and shoved his hands into his pant pockets. "Fine," he said. "Come on in. Be a jerk."

He followed me up the stairs, down the hall, around a corner, and into his studio. Drew was sitting on the edge of Mason's worktable, surrounded by piles and piles of magazine pictures. He was naked, extremely hazy about the eyes, and polka-dotted with hickeys and bite marks. His hair was a mess, and he did have a slightly weird forehead, now that I'd noticed it. You could see the contours of his skull, for one thing. When Drew saw me, he grinned. I think he intended the grin to look sly, but it wasn't. That part of his personality was gone. Maybe that whack on the head had destroyed it. Maybe I'd only imagined it. Anyway, he just looked like a fourteen-year-old who was involved in some sexual trip that was none of my business.

"Are you okay?" I asked.

"Yeah," Drew said. The grin crumbled under the pressure of some kind of head pain that made him twist up his face like an air heavy-metal guitarist.

"See?" said Mason's voice. It was somewhere behind me.

"But he hit you."

"I know," Drew said. Then another pain totalled his face. "But he told me why he did it, and . . . I understand, and . . . I'm cool with it." He tried to grin.

"See?" said Mason's voice.

When I got home, there was a message from Luke on my answering machine. It said he was home, packing up his belongings, and to give him a call. I sat down at the desk and tried to reorganize my identity, first by closing my eyes, which didn't quite work, then by looking very hard at my bulletin board, not at the page with the wish but at the pictures of beautiful boys all around it. At first they meant nothing to me. All I could think was, My type's so specific. Then I got kind of snagged on the picture of Smear, on the Alex Johns part of it. I hadn't thought about him since that weird scene at Mason's. Whatever I'd seen in his beauty was gone. I mean, the beauty itself was completely unaffected and sterling, but my attachment was vague. It's hard to describe. Point is, the indifference made me feel sane, which was nice.

"Luke?" I asked when he answered.

"Oh, hi," he said. "Let me . . . turn down the stereo." The phone clunked and filled with a skittery electronic music. The music dimmed, and the phone clunked again. "Hi. What's going on?"

"Not much," I said. "I've been running some errands. You?"

"Take a guess," he said, mock-exasperated. "I can't wait to get out of here. My roommate's upset about me moving out, so it's kind of uncomfortable."

"What, do you owe him rent?"

"No, he just likes me a lot, I guess. It's weird."

"You don't like him that much?"

"No, he's cool. But I'm not *upset*."

"So what did you want to talk to me about?"

"Oh, right. Okay . . . I hope you won't be offended."

"Gulp."

"What?"

"It sounds heavy."

"No, no. It's just because I'm moving in with you, and . . . I hope this doesn't sound cold, but I know I'm your type, and I just don't want you to have any hopes that something's going to happen between us."

It was weird. I felt so drained all of a sudden. "Yeah, I know," I said.

"Because the way you look at me sometimes . . . It doesn't bother me. I mean, I like it in a way, but I don't want you to—"

"I don't."

"But you're attracted to me."

"Yeah, but—"

"And . . . I read what you wrote about me. You know, on your bulletin board."

I looked up at the board. There it was, my wish, written out in a drug-addled script. *I wish Luke would fall in love with me.* "Oh, yeah," I said.

"So you can see why I'm worried."

"Yeah."

"You know?"

"Yeah, look . . ." Then I thought about everything in the world for a second. "I'm a weird, fucked-up person," I said. "I know that. There are all kinds of things that I wish could be true that I know can't be true. And the truth is, I'm so fucked up that there's no way that anyone could fall in love with me, even if he wanted to. Even if someone said he was in love with me, it wouldn't be true, because there are parts of me that I don't understand, and that I can't talk about, because I would just sound insane. So even if someone did fall in love with the part of me that I'm able to show to the world, I wouldn't believe it."

I heard Luke think. It wasn't a sound, just a vibe.

"Besides, since you read the wish, it won't work anyway, right? Isn't that how the magic thing works?"

"I'm afraid so." He cleared his throat. Or, rather, mock-cleared it.

"So you're off the hook," I said. Then I got an idea, reached up, pried the yellow pushpin from the wish, and positioned the page in front of me on the desk.

"That's cool," Luke said. "Well, I don't mean it's cool, but . . . you know what I mean. It's just not . . . possible."

"But I thought anything was possible." I slid a pen from the can full of pencils and pens, studied the page for a second, then scratched out the words *fall in* and *with*. Then I read the new sentence a couple of times, realized I could live with the changes, and thumbtacked the page to the bulletin board. "Look, I'm kidding," I added. "It's fine. Don't worry about it. It was just a thought."

"Are you sure?"

"Yeah. In fact, I just made a different wish while we were talking."

"Cool. Is it about me?"

"Yeah," I said. "But it's much more realistic."

After we hung up, I stared at the rewritten wish. Then I worked on the novel. This chapter, specifically. That was pretty much it. I sat around and wrote. At some point I took a break, slid the Polaroid from my pocket, and studied the look, or lack of look, on Sniffles's new, wizened face. Whatever he felt nowadays, it seemed huge. I couldn't begin to describe it. Anyway, its largesse made me realize that beating him up wasn't that big a deal by comparison. He was on to much bigger, much weirder things. So was I. I was probably thinking of Mason and Drew and all that. Then I started to sob. I guess I was tired. I cried about this and that terrible thing for the next several hours. It's sort of a blur now. I know I was stumbling around the apartment, falling down on the floor, yelling, screaming, unable to think straight or even, at some points, see clearly. I imagine the freak-out revolved around Luke. I know that having sex fucks me up, and that romantic love is just an intellectual construct, but part of me, however idiotic, had hoped that Luke and I might delude each other. I think we would have been happy together. I can't prove that obviously. Point is, I felt sort of hopeless, and when I dwelled on that thought for too long I'd go off. Occasionally I'd sense how absurd I was acting and calm down a bit. During one little lull I had a strange realization. I.e., that the only difference between this crying jag and the one I'd experienced back in my acid-flamed teens was the absence of someone like Craig. I'd completely forgotten that aspect. You know, that he'd been there guiding me back. Maybe if someone that thoughtful and warm had been in my apartment, I would have returned to the real world a much saner, less complex man. Does that make sense? I probably should have taken some notes at the time. But I was much too chaotic to transcribe my thoughts without spewing out self-involved gibberish. And now that I'm fine, loneliness is far too heavy and painful a state to relive. Still, I'm pretty sure it's the truth. I'm completely alone. Not to raise my solitude over anyone else's. It's just scary sometimes. That's all I can say about that. Sorry it's vague.

The *Spin* Article

The Onyx Café is an East Hollywood coffeehouse decorated with clumsy neo-Expressionist paintings and usually half-packed with bohemian trendoids. It's early afternoon. David, an HIV-positive street prostitute, has agreed to share a few days of his endangered young life if I promise to plug his band. They're called the Rambo Dolls, and more on them later. That's David storming in the entrance. I can just tell.

With his long, tangled blond hair, bony face, huge blue eyes, and grunge garb—holey jeans, Sandy Duncan's Eye T-shirt, untucked flannels, scuffed Docs, David looks like a rock star, specifically Soul Asylum's Dave Pirner. But once he joins me at my table, and I get a closer look, his face is almost scary. The thing's just a little too perfectly constructed. Not that anxiety doesn't radiate from every detail. Still, it's weird to think that someone this conventionally cute could be homeless.

"How did you get infected?"

"Well, it was either from sharing needles with people I didn't know," he says, staring at his lap, "or from letting guys fuck me without a condom, or from fucking girls I knew had AIDS without a condom. I could've been infected a hundred times, you know?" He pauses, and his stare grows extremely forlorn. "Do you think that makes a difference?" He looks up at me for a second. "I mean, that I could've gotten infected a lot?"

I don't know what to say. From what I hear, repeated exposures do complicate the infection. But I'm still so distracted and cowed by David's looks that I just sort of stammer that he should, like, be careful.

"Yeah, obviously!" All around us, people peer at him over their books. "I mean, I already should've been . . . more . . ." Suddenly he twists around in his chair. "Go *away*! *Do* something!"

Every head turns. A scrawny redheaded woman, maybe twenty-six, dressed in a scuffed bomber jacket and jeans, is standing just outside the Onyx's doorway. "All right, *all right*," she yells back, and blurs out of sight to the right.

"Your . . . girlfriend?"

David untwists. "Yeah," he says. "Dora. I'm crashing at her place right now. She's all right, she's just . . . she wants me to love her and I told her I can't because I'm going to die, but she still wants me to, so . . ." He cringes.

"That's a tough one."

He nods violently. "And she's a heroin junkie too," he continues, slumping down in the chair. "That's fucked up because I'm off everything now since the HIV thing. So I have to watch her shoot up all the time and it's . . . fucked. But I never liked heroin, so it's easier than if she was doing crystal or something I used to like. But it makes her hard to deal with, you know?" His expression is growing increasingly hangdog, his eyes, unfocused, on what looks like a petrified muffin crumb on the table between us.

"I'm sure," I say. "Anyway, what's this about your rock band?"

"Oh, fuck." He tenses, kicks his chair back from the table, and shoots me a horrified look. The Onyx populace, which had

just relaxed back into their books, are all eyes, not that David realizes or cares. "Now I have to live up to it, right?" he says. "Maybe
you should just come see us rehearse later, like I said. Then you
can decide if . . ." He shrugs.

With organizations like Covenant House, Angel's Flight, the
Gay and Lesbian Center, and others concentrating their efforts
on easing the plight of young runaways, you'd think the situation
was under control—to some degree, at least. I did. Not according
to David. He's avoided such places whenever he can, although he
can't quite explain his aversion. He doesn't want to be "con-
trolled," is the short and long of it. According to him, even the
most religion-free outreach program has some sort of freedom-
obliterating agenda. Instead, he has these floating parental-type
figures. In the past, he'd relied on a series of regular johns whose
concern for his welfare was just real enough to feel nice and just
suspicious enough to be rejected guilt-free. Nowadays he relies on
immediate friends, several of whom I'll meet later this day, and
most of whom read as caretaker types, as the therapists say—boys
and girls whose devotion to David's welfare has a slightly hysteri-
cal edge.

We're leaning on a parked car just outside the Onyx. Half a
block up the street, Dora keeps yo-yo-ing in and out of a bookshop,
neck craned—checking our status, I guess. I let David blab about
whatever he wants. Mostly he rags on the Onyx clientele and how,
well, artsy-fartsiness is the opiate of the new bourgeoisie, basically.
Classic punk stuff.
David may be a semi–emotional wreck, but he's sharp, albeit in a kneejerk, self-taught kind of way. According to him, his
politics, philosophy, and musical tastes were formed by the brainy
punk magazine *Maximum Rock 'n' Roll*, which he's been reading

religiously since he was a kid. Now that we're in the daylight, I can see that he has shoved between his belt and jeans a freshly shoplifted book by cultural theorist Noam Chomsky, MR'n'R's unoffical guru. He's been meaning to dip into Chomsky since his pre-diagnosis, pre-homeless days, meaning four months ago.

Back then he lived with a bunch of other quasi-anarchist teen squatters in an abandoned building off Hollywood Boulevard. He'll talk about that roughly yearlong period of his life in great detail, but the time before then—in other words, his entire childhood and adolescence—is interviewer non grata. When he accidentally lets a detail slip—that he grew up in the San Fernando Valley, or that his father is a doctor—it's accompanied by a physical explosion. The air's punched, the sidewalk's stomped. When I press him, all David will admit about his past is that whatever happened, which is none of my business, it made him realize how people don't give a shit for each other, no matter what they say.

"What about your friends?"

"Right," David says. "Well, I don't keep them very long. Most of my friends aren't real friends, they're just guys who are into me sexually. But when they realize what an asshole I am, and that I'm never going to let them fuck me, they're gone."

"Why don't you just let them fuck you? I mean, you're a hustler, so—"

"Because they're my *friends*," he yells. Then he looks away, smiles sort of weirdly, and clears his throat. "You're into me too, aren't you?"

"No," I say. And I'm not, actually.

David glances up. His smile grows all fake and flirtatious. "Oh, yeah, right."

I know that smile. Two of my boyfriends were part-time street hustlers, as were most of their friends. In the days before AIDS, I used to hang around hustler bars, sometimes intending to pick up a boy but more often than not just because I enjoyed the tension. I've been given the hard sell by hustlers on hundreds of occasions, and David's obviously . . . well, if not an expert, then a veteran. Add that semi-expertise to his beauty, and he must do pretty well in that underworld. True?

"True," he agrees, and laughs uproariously. "But it's not like I'm spending my last days on earth in some rich scumbag's mansion." According to him, he's had innumerable chances to "sell out," as he puts it, particularly with "a famous record-company executive" whom he won't name, partly because the guy still rents him out on occasion and partly because he's respectful of other people's privacy. "But I guess if I was really considerate," he says, "I'd still be living in the squat, and not with a fucking junkie." He shoots a murderous glare up the sidewalk. "Dora! Get your ass down here! Let's go!"

Desire is so weird. I'm not attracted to David in any real kind of way. If this were, say, the very early eighties, pre–AIDS recognition, when I'd occasionally get lonely or overaesthetic re sex and cruise L.A.'s hustler strip, then maybe snag some specimen off a low-lit street corner, David would look really good. But in today's poisoned context, availability and looks aren't enough. Besides, something about David spooks me. I'm into sweetness, even if it's superficially lost in some cute guy's confusion or fear or paranoia. But not when it's lost in hostility. And David is borderline explosive, as I hope I've made clear. Still, I live in my head, as you're aware, and reality doesn't necessarily impinge on my wishes. In that realm, the boy's suitable, to say the least. So as we walk to my car, David arguing with Dora, he's secretly the object of a modest mental orgy.

†

I'm driving David and Dora to her downtown apartment, where the Rambo Dolls have arranged a rehearsal. At my request, David directs us along Hollywood Boulevard, pointing out haunts from his days in the squat. In a spot near Mann's Chinese Theater that he has just called "the world's greatest panhandling area," he notices one of his friends, a former squatmate, now the lead singer in their band.

Sniffles is a tall, slim late teen with an exotic face, sleepy brown eyes, surly lips, and a filthy blond mohawk that sags down one side of his head. Dressed in jeans, a denim jacket, and an old, faded Tom Verlaine T-shirt, he's accosting passersby with his hand out when David orders me over to the curb.

"Hey, shit sack!" David yells, shoving his head and shoulders through the open passenger window. He topples out onto the sidewalk. Sniffles helps him up, and they half hug, half wrestle, for a few minutes, while tourists veer around them.

Inside the car, Dora and I watch, trading bemused smiles. Assuming David's telling me the truth about her addiction, she's jonesing pretty badly. Her face is greenish white. Her pupils are gigantic. Her skinny arms are practically strangling her upper torso. "David's . . . such a . . . liar," she says, teeth chattering, watching the boys mock-battle.

"How so?" I'm watching them too.

"Like when he says he doesn't love me," she says. "I'm sure he told you that. But I put up with his bullshit. Nobody else ever did. He's a lot sicker than he says he is. You can't see it that much, but he's really fucking thin, and he's got diarrhea all the time now. That's why he doesn't hustle very much anymore. So when—"

Suddenly the car door opens, and David hurls himself inside, squashing Dora against me, and me against my door. Sniffles joins us, slamming the door shut behind him.

"Greetings." The new boy smirks.

"Two things." David's face is about an inch from mine. I can smell AZT on his breath. "First, you can give Sniffles a ride, right?" It's kind of a sour chemical stink that doesn't fit with his being at all. "And, okay, secondly he wants to know if you feel like fucking him for not very much money at all. Dora and I can take the bus. I mean, that's cool. Then you guys can meet us at Dora's later for the rehearsal. Because I told him you're a . . ." David's eyes get confused. ". . . queer? Is that what you guys want to be called now? Because he's queer, too, and he's a nice guy, and he's broke, right?" David eyeballs me, Sniffles, me, Sniffles . . .

After the couple heads off, I take Sniffles to lunch at a nearby coffee shop, and he tells me his story, which is as heavily censored as David's. The way these guys edit their past, you'd think they had no adolescence at all. As for the present, he mostly panhandles, smokes pot, sings for the Rambo Dolls, and hustles. Hustling makes him depressed, he says, maybe because, being queer, he expects too much love from his johns or whatever. Unlike David, he'll utilize Covenant House when there's no other option. For him it's a practical thing, i.e., it's worth a little lecture and psychological bullshit to sleep in a bed. At the time of our talk, he was still commandeering a room in the Hollywood squat where David lived for a while. After lunch, we take a drive over there.

We enter a onetime Victorian mansion that has clearly been through several subsequent lives as an apartment building. Its fanciness is smashed, weathered, and dirtied into a baroque cave. Most of the squat's current residents are away at the moment, hanging out on the Boulevard, panhandling for fast-food and drug cash, but there's a young heterosexual couple, maybe fourteen years old, playing cards in the immense living room. They have innocent faces and dated punk haircuts, they wear several layers of threadbare black clothes, and their B.O. trails all the way up to the second story, where Sniffles shows me his room, a small walk-in closet. Mattress, tangled blanket, a small hill of clothing. He sits down in the middle, studies his crotch for a second, then smiles up at me. One of those smiles. Oh, shit.

"So who gets to live in the squat?" I ask, trying to avoid his gaze.

"Anybody," he says. "You just have to be honest, and not too strung out. And you can't fuck around with our stuff."

"I take it David broke the rules."

"Every one of them. I fought for him. And we almost let him stay, because he's so fucking beautiful."

"So, are you *into* David?"

His smile sort of generalizes. Phew. "And I'm going to get him," he says.

"Don't be so sure."

"Oh, I will. And if he fights it, then fuck him. I'll never speak to him again. But he needs me, so I'm not worried." Then Sniffles's smile gets all seductive again. Only this time his target's a day-dream. "I'm just waiting for the right moment."

Have I made it obvious that I'm attracted to Sniffles? Probably not, since fucking him would be quite unethical—theoretically, at least. Not that I've been able to figure out why it's unethical. Anyway, Sniffles is making it very, very sticky for me, because he's so up my alley. At first I just thought he was sweet, no big deal. I guess that's why I didn't emphasize his beauty early on. But by the time we'd arrived at the squat, I was borderline infatuated with him. And Sniffles obviously knew how I felt. And I was pretty sure that he knew that I knew that he knew.

†

With a rough little head shake, Sniffles exits his daydream. His eyes target me and re-warm. Or I can feel their strange heat again. "So . . ." he says quietly. "What about us doing something?"

"What about it?" I'm sure he realizes I'm weakening. Not to generalize, but hustlers intuit these things. Anyway, it's probably obvious. Unlike David, I don't have a face you can hide thoughts behind. Mine's all rubbery.

"Shut the door," Sniffles says. His smile has grown incredibly dense—like a psychic's or something.

"When's your rehearsal again?" I'm fully aware that my question's a yes in sheep's clothing.

"In a while." Sniffles sucks in a breath, holds it down for a second or two—like he's just taken a big hit of pot—then exhales very slowly and noisily. As he does, his body relaxes into a state I can only describe as available. "What can you afford?" he adds.

"Oh, fuck off." And I laugh.

"There are a couple of things I won't do," he adds, studying me. "You can probably guess what they are."

"You don't kiss."

"That's one of them, yeah." And Sniffles's smile sort of . . . weakens? "But . . . you're nice, so . . ."

Hustlers who give a shit about anyone else are unbelievably rare, in my experience. They're practically a delicacy. When in the old days I sensed interest in a hustler, I bought. I mean, if the guy was my physical type to begin with. No second thoughts. Because with that extra ingredient, you're almost guaranteed memorable sex. One hustler I bought had this mini–nervous breakdown right there in my arms. I've had hustlers claim they've fallen deeply in love with me. They've burst into tears, asked me to adopt them, marry them, confessed all variety of personal trauma. The looks in their eyes can get out of this world. I'm talking sex so realistic that when it comes time to pay them, it doesn't even matter. I've had hustlers refuse to take money, as if they thought one selfless act could make somebody love them. Things can get grim, but it's incredibly hot in the moment.

"Oh, all right."

"Awesome." Sniffles lies back and smirks at the ceiling. "What do you like to do?" His fists are pounding out a rhythm on the mattress.

To get decent sex out of hustlers, you need to list your preferences right away. It relaxes them and helps you organize your attack. In description, my little fetish for eating out, spanking, exploring, and fucking guys' asses sounds easy to cope with. One's just expected to go with the flow. Thing is, the sex can get very disconcerting in its own funny way. Some boys grow uptight, especially if they don't like their own bodies. I mean, I get *in there*. But like I said, in theory it sounds like a lark.

"That'll work," Sniffles says, fiddling with his belt. "Let's talk money later on."

"Wait a second." I'm famous for these little last-minute anxiety attacks. Or I would be famous for them if the people I fucked had any clout in the world. "Can we do it at my place?" Maybe it's just the unusual locale. "It's on the way downtown."

Sniffles quits fiddling. "Awesome," he says.

When we exit the mansion, David and Dora are out on the sidewalk arguing loudly with some grisly punk kid. He must be a squat resident since Sniffles mumbles a name, maybe Fred, with this slight exasperation, then jets on ahead of me, skidding to a halt along their periphery. He adds his yell to their yells, defend-

ing David, I'm not sure against what. They sound like the punk-
rock equivalent of a barbershop quartet. Still, it feels dangerous,
so I wait in the car. From what I can tell, Sniffles's support just
infuriates David. He backs away from the group, screaming at them
to fuck off. Then he whirls around and runs up the street. Sniffles
shouts David's name and takes off after him, leaving Dora to squall
at the punk on her own. Halfway down the block, Sniffles catches
up with David and grabs a fistful of his T-shirt. David whips around,
shoves Sniffles down on the ground, and takes off. Sniffles stands
up, yells something at David, then turns and starts to limp in my
general direction, rubbing one knee. When he sees me in the car,
he breaks into a lopsided trot.

"Let's go," he says, throwing open the passenger door. He
slams it behind him. "Fuck David." Then he winces at me. "I didn't
mean that."

"I know."

"We should zoom." Sniffles turns and looks behind us. Dora
is gone, and the grisly punk is eyeballing our car.

I drive off. It's one of those weird, smog-beautified L.A. late
afternoons. Sniffles slumps in the seat, blinking at the taillights
and lushly colored daylight before us. He looks much more freaked
out than he did a few minutes ago. It's strange how when people
are frightened they seem to grow younger, especially if they look
like overgrown kids to begin with. Sniffles looks about twelve.
"David'll be okay," I say.

"I guess." Sniffles turns and looks at me really, really hard.

"What?"

"You're cool, but there's something . . . I don't know, weird
about you."

"I know. I think so too."

Sniffles stares out the windshield for several minutes, watching neighborhoods change into other kinds of neighborhoods. I guess they're gentrifying the closer we get to my own. I never think about things like that. "So you're into kissing," he says without looking at me.

"I didn't say that."

Sniffles checks me out, his eyes charged with a thought that I'm far too excited about to begin to decode. "I don't know," he says. "That's sort of the one thing I'm really not into." Then he cringes, like he's sure I'll say no.

"How about this," I say. "No kissing, but anything else is okay, and I'll give you . . . I don't know, five hundred dollars, if it's really amazing."

Sniffles's eyes freak. They practically electrocute me, the road ahead, his own crotch. "Shit, *yeah*," he shouts. "Whatever you want to do. That's . . . *wow*." He slides low in the seat, rests his Docs on the dashboard, and starts pounding out a rhythm on his knees. "Are you rich? Because you don't seem rich."

"No. I'm just spending *Spin*'s expense account."

"Great scam."

"I guess."

"So when you say 'amazing,' what do you mean?"

"Well, you're amazing."

He smiles cautiously. "I'm your type."

"Completely."

"That's cool," he says. He thinks for a second. "Yeah, that's really cool. I like you too. I have a thing for older guys. And I sort of like being told what to do. During sex, I mean, not in my life."

"Lucky me."

Sniffles studies my eyes. "So what's your thing? You want to fuck me without a condom? I mean, that's no problem, if you want to."

"No, no. God, you shouldn't do that."

"Yeah, I know." Sniffles grins. "Oh, I know what you're thinking."

"What?"

Sniffles stifles the grin, but it's still there, just stunted. "You want to hit me."

"Actually, I wasn't—" But now that he mentions it. Well, not "hit." That's not a word I would use. I might have said "rough." "Rough" sounds more . . . something.

"You can tell I'm into that, right?" Sniffles says. "Johns always know. They never even ask, they just start whaling on me."

I picture that scene for a few seconds. "Yeah, I could tell." Like Sniffles says, I'm weird.

"Wacky." He fixes his eyes on something far beyond the windshield. "I don't know why, but I love when guys hit me. I guess it's because of my dad or whatever. It's like my favorite fucking thing in the world."

"Lucky me," I say.

Sniffles's eyes search mine. "Cool, yeah. Listen, is there any possibility . . ." he says, smiling, ". . . that we could . . . have a relationship?"

"You mean, like boyfriends."

"Not the normal, boring kind of boyfriends. I mean, because I'm in love with David, you know? I just mean . . . not like a sugar daddy or anything. Maybe sort of like a father-figure type who'll beat the shit out of me when I'm feeling fucked up. That's sort of a huge fantasy."

"It's possible." I guess it is, although very remotely. Anyway, we're home. "That's the place." And I point.

My apartment is more like a very small one-story house, with bread-box ceilings and pink window shades, set among five almost identical units in a small tree-lined court. Sniffles immediately gives himself a tour. I pour him a large glass of scotch on the rocks, at his request. He stops at my CD collection, chooses Television's *Adventure*, and slips it into the player just about the time I return with his drink and all the drugs I have stashed in the house. A few hits of Ecstasy, some tranquilizers, a gram of crystal meth. I've been saving them up on the off chance some weird situation would arise. This is definitely that. See, if I really go wild like I do in my daydreams, Sniffles will need some chemical interference. And I half explain this to him, in so many words. For better or worse, he's already stoned insensible by the prospect of five hundred dollars and/or the effect of his slight crush on me. So he washes down the three hits of Ecstasy, fakes a satisfied burp, and relaxes back into the couch, shooting me these debauched little looks. I settle into an armchair, snort a few lines of crystal, volley his increasingly disoriented blather, and wait for the drugs to distort me. It takes about twenty-five minutes.

It's ninety minutes later. I'm sitting on the foot of the bed, jittering in the feeble last rays of the crystal. Sniffles is sprawled out behind me, still jerking off. He can't seem to find the right moment. His face is elongated over a daydream, presumably violent. I don't know where he is, but I guess I'm involved. My come's caking up on his stomach and chest. His lips are twice their old size, slightly crooked, smeared with blood, and sort of starry with bits of saliva. One eye's purplish and swelling shut as I watch. If I could see his ass, I'm positive it would look thrashed. If Sniffles hadn't just stopped me, I don't know what would have happened. His face was so blurred by my slaps that I didn't even notice the blood. Then he grabbed my wrist. That woke me up. "Blood," he said. He could hardly pronounce that. I.e., if there was a virus in him, it was loose. Still, that didn't scare me as much as my thoughts. I really wanted to kill him.

I really thought that he'd let me. So I threw myself here. I'd come twice, but I guess I was thinking of going for three. He keeps saying, "Amazing," just under his breath. It is and it isn't, obviously. That could be the Ecstasy talking. I'm waiting for him to come back to reality, so we can communicate. And a few seconds later, he comes. When Sniffles comes, he yells—I mean, loudly—like his dick is a band that has just started playing his favorite song. It's a good thing my neighbors are never around.

"My mind works like this," David is saying. We're standing in the narrow hallway outside Dora's apartment. She's inside, shooting up. Sniffles is at the corner store, stealing us a six-pack. "Usually, I don't think about having AIDS. I mean about having HIV. I always forget that it's not technically AIDS yet. But then when I do remember, this is what happens. It's usually right after I've had sex with somebody—not Dora, so much, but with men who pay me. I think, I have HIV, okay, but it'll be fine. The doctor says I have maybe ten years from the time I got infected before I die if I take care of myself. But then I think, Well, I could've gotten infected seven years ago, because I've been letting guys fuck me since I was twelve, as weird as that sounds. Then I think how many drugs I've done, and what that's probably done to my immune system. And I start to get really scared, and I think, Fuck it. I'm going to kill myself now before I get sick. Because it's too much, you know? Then I think, I hate everybody. Somebody gave this to me. You can't trust anyone. And I get so tense that I want to kill people, and my friends get shit from me because they're there. And then I get really guilty about treating my friends shitty, so I apologize to them, and they're usually okay about it. And that's a relief. So I feel better, and I've sort of forgotten about the AIDS. So my mind's made this weird journey to get me away from thinking I have AIDS—I mean, HIV. Do you think it does that consciously? Do you know what I mean?"

David always asks these impossible questions. Luckily, his attention span sucks, and he immediately slugs Dora's door. "Wake up, you fucking pincushion!"

Minutes later, the rest of the Rambo Dolls show. Warren is a tall, polite African American in his early twenties. Six months ago, a friend bought him an hour of David's services as a joke birthday gift, and the two became friends. A bass player, he's the only Rambo Doll with a smidgen of technical prowess. Brett, guitarist, is a hippie-esque sixteen-year-old, newly off drugs, and a born-again Christian. He doesn't say much. He's brought along a crappy little amp, which he shares with Warren. David, drummer, can't afford a kit, so he perches on the edge of Dora's bed with a coffee-table art book in his lap and a pencil in each fist.

Over the next, oh, hour and a half, David thwacks the book so violently that he spars with the general din. As far as I can tell from the Rambo Dolls' lurching sketch of a sound, the music's parochial hardcore. Sort of like if the Shaggs had grown up listening to the Melvins. Sniffles, fat-lipped and black-eyed from my beating, limps around the room singing/yelling some punkified lyrics re misogyny, racism, drug use, et cetera. Studying these Little Rascals–esque antics, I feel kind of sad, truth be told. Fortunately, they're oblivious. It's only after Brett and Warren have left, and Sniffles is napping, that David nervously asks what I thought, by which time I'm mentally ready to lie. "Very cool," I say.

"Thanks," David says happily. Dora's sprawled in his lap, nodding out. "Yeah, I think in a year we'll be famous. That's my goal."

"How famous?"

"As famous as . . . and as good as . . . Sandy Duncan's Eye."

"But they're not very famous," I say. I'm beginning to see what Dora meant. In the sharp window light, David's face does reveal a bit too much skull.

"They're famous enough," he says.

"Why not as famous as U2?"

David goggles at me. "Because they suck."

"Okay, but why not be in a great band that happens to be really famous?"

He looks horrified. "Impossible, man."

"Then what else? Other life goals, I mean."

"To not die. Not for a long time." He glances at Dora, then smiles conspiratorially at me. "And . . . have a great girlfriend," he half whispers, then checks to see if she's awake. Nope. "And be rich . . . somehow." Now he's crowing again. "And never see my parents again. Uh . . . be a great drummer."

"Do you have a favorite drummer?"

"Adam Pfahler."

"Who's in . . ."

"Jawbreaker. Fuck, they're *great*. Okay, I want my band to be as famous as Jawbreaker. And as good as them."

"Jawbreaker's more famous than Sandy Duncan's Eye? I guess they are."

"Well, Jawbreaker's known for being brilliant. But Sandy Duncan's Eye is more known for their weird name. So it would be better to be like Jawbreaker." He shoots me a grin that makes him look about seven years old. Suddenly it decays into a grimace, and he punches the air. "But I'm going to die soon anyway, so . . . who cares?" He glares into space for a second, then shoves Dora off him. She hits the floor, thwack, not too far away from Sniffles, rolls slowly onto her side, and winces up at David with this deep if very foggy concern.

"Shit," she slurs. "Are you . . . crying, David?"

And, yeah, fuck, he is.

I'm sitting on the bed, hugging David. His face is smashed into my neck, just below the right ear. Occasionally he sobs, and we jolt. I've been stroking his hair for a couple of minutes. Dora is struggling to stay in the world, but the heroin's swallowing her, eyelids first. Sniffles is a log.

"David," I say. "Come on, let's go for a walk."

"Fuck," he says, voice all screechy. "Fuck, fuck . . ." And he struggles to his feet.

I follow him out the door, down the hall, into the stairwell, up a few flights, then through a metal door that puts us out on the roof. Too bad downtown Los Angeles is such a total pit, because you can see for miles.

"I just don't know anymore," David says. He's racing around on the roof. "What do you think I should do?"

"About what?" I ask. Because I'm not sure. I mean, he has so many problems.

"About *AIDS*," he says. Actually, he yells. "I have *AIDS*. It's not just HIV. I've fucking *got* it. Shit's *happening* to me."

"All you can do is take care of yourself." It sounds facile, but really, what else can you say?

"It's not helping," he says. "I've fucked up my body too much. It can't do anything by itself. And I can't . . . *can't* stay with Dora. She makes me too tense, and that isn't . . ." He shuts up and wanders around for a while. When David walks, he stomps the ground—or, in this case, the roof—as if every step were important to him, and his long, messy hair flaps around his handsome head in slow, rickety motion like the wings of some huge, sloppy bird. "So," he mumbles. "You did it with Sniffles."

"Yeah."

"You really fucked him. How much did it cost you?"

For whatever reason, I fudge. I guess I don't want to seem too unprofessional and/or pathetic. "Two hundred and fifty dollars."

He stops walking and gawps at me. "You're fucking joking."

"Nope."

"Two hundred and fifty dollars?" And his eyes jet all over the place. Sky, roof, me. Then I think he tries to smile, but it doesn't quite focus. "Shit, I'd even do you for two hundred and fifty dollars." I don't have a clue what that does to my face, but assuming it shows what I feel, which is "Uh-oh," David can't seem to translate. "That's an offer," he adds. "You can't hit me, but anything else is okay."

I'm weird, okay? I don't know if I'm a saint, or if I'm scared of confrontation, or if I'm incredibly fucked-up and selfish. Hence, my going back through this encounter and recounting it in as faithful a manner as possible. I know I don't want to fuck David, not just because he has AIDS. Maybe if he wasn't infected, or if I was high, I could get into, say, tying him up and all that. You know, taming the wild beast, et cetera. Anyway, I can't explain my response.

"Well, I'd have to hit an ATM."

"Later," he says. Unlike Sniffles, he doesn't look happy at all. His eyes are scouring the roof. "We can do it in there," he says, and heads toward the metal door. "What are you into?"

I'm following. "I don't know." Actually I do, just not with him.

"Bullshit, " David says. He hurls open the door.

We're standing on a landing, maybe five feet by eight. The floor's very scummy and slick. A dusty red lightbulb pops out of one wall, casting this pornoesque glow. Stairs plunge to my immediate left, to David's right. David has whipped off his T-shirt and is shoving his jeans to his ankles. He has the sort of body that must have been perfect the day he was born—broad-shouldered,

narrow-hipped, completely smooth, with a lengthy, fat dick and a
small, boxy ass. If AIDS is destroying him, he's holding his own
pretty well. Of course, the lack of light helps.

"Come on," he says impatiently. He's naked now. One hand
is working violently on his dick. The other is pointing for me to
undress.

"You're beautiful," I say, just to say something.

"Oh, shit. Don't say that." David looks down the stairs and
kind of winces.

"But I really don't know what to do."

"Anything you *want*," he yells. "Shit." He looks down at his
dick, which isn't the slightest bit hard, and pumps faster, his eyes
sort of begging it.

"Let's not, okay? I'll just give you some money."

"I know you're into me."

"I'm not." I'm really not.

"Okay," he says. I've just noticed the crooked little teardrop
on his cheek. "But do you mind if I come? I promise I won't get
any on you."

"No, no. I don't mind."

"Thanks. You don't have to pay me." He takes a step back
and leans against the wall, then jerks off, looking at me very intently. Maybe it's a trick of the teardrops, but I can see some desire in his eyes. I don't know what's going on in his head, obviously,
and I doubt I'm directly involved, but my proximity's making a
difference, I guess. Anyway, he's hard.

"What are you thinking about?"

"I don't know." He looks startled, and checks the stairs.
"About not being alone."

"Do you mind if I jerk off too?" I guess his beauty's affecting
me. That and my sympathy for him. And my weird imagination.

"No, that'd be good," he says.

†

In my fantasy, David is jerking off in my bed. I've made him very gentle and stoned. We're picking up from where I left off with Sniffles. First I bash in his face. Then I pick up a knife, pry his hand off his dick, take ahold of his genitals, give them a yank, slice them free at the root, and drop them into his mouth. Now I'm stabbing him in the stomach and chest. Blood is spraying all over the place. I'll get HIV, but that's karma. My sacrifice makes David's death seem so intense, I can't tell you. He's ready, I'm just about ready. I bend his legs back, slide my dick up what's left of his ass, put the tip of the knife to the centermost point of his throat, then fuck him hard and slowly bury the blade.

I notice it first. A solid, wobbling patch of . . . something, I'm not exactly sure what, in the dark at the foot of the stairs. "David," I say, and stuff my hard-on back into my pants.

David unscrunches his eyes. They're dazed. It's nice. "Did you come?" He studies the floor by my shoes. "Just a second. I'm . . . almost . . ."

"Someone's watching." I recheck the patch.

David squints down the staircase. "Oh, shit." He immediately bends down and grabs at his clothes.

Sniffles runs up the stairs. "What are you guys doing?" he shouts. "As if I didn't fucking know." He stops short on the top step, coughing and rubbing his eyes very gently. "Oh, man, head rush."

David has already stepped into his jeans and is dragging them up over his thighs. "Fuck off," he mumbles.

Sniffles grins and points. "I saw your cock, I saw your cock." He turns to me. "Do you know how long I've been waiting to see his cock?" He turns to David. "I bet he's not paying you as much as he paid me."

"Where's Dora?" David has his T-shirt back on and is untangling the flannels.

"Losing her shit down there."

"Cool," David says.

"Yeah, totally." Sniffles's eyes leave David's body and smash into mine. I expect to see jealousy, maybe even betrayal, but all I can read is lovesickness. It looks like pain. And I guess I must care about him, or feel some delayed guilt, at least, because my throat starts to ache very slightly.

"David," I say, but I'm looking at Sniffles, whose reaction is paramount. "If I paid you five hundred dollars, would you do it with Sniffles?"

Sniffles's eyes do that explosion thing, like his pupils are the bottoms of rockets blasting off into his irises.

David slams his back against the wall and looks up at the ceiling. "You mean, to watch us?" He lets out a big, smelly breath. "Or do you mean you want to fuck us both?"

I check in with Sniffles. His face has this scared, back-pedaling, faraway sort of post-slap expression. So I take a guess. "To do whatever Sniffles wants you to do."

"*Fuck* no," David yells. "If I start hitting him, I'll fucking kill him. I can't do shit like that. I'm too crazy."

"You can kill me," Sniffles says, smiling. I guess or I hope that's a joke.

David turns on Sniffles. "You're fucked up, man. No way." He looks at me, imploringly, I think. "No way. Look . . . shit, if you tell us what to do, then . . . okay, okay, whatever."

I try Sniffles's eyes. They're warm. "Deal."

"Fuck, fuck, fuck . . . Let's do it down there," David says. "I'll throw Dora out." And he charges down the stairs.

As soon as David turns the corner, Sniffles sneaks me a grin. "You're so fucking cool," he whispers. "Tell David you want us to act like we're lovers." Then he tears down the stairs.

†

"Get out," David says. He waves at the door. We're in Dora's place, obviously. He means her.

Dora hasn't been told anything, but she knows. Actually, she probably thinks I want to fuck the two boys. She's on the bed. "All right, David," she says, and struggles to her feet. "You know," she adds, "you're like that guy in *The Time Machine*." At first I think she means David, which I don't quite understand, but then her eyes target me. "*You*, asshole. You're fucking everything up, and you don't even know it." Then she stumbles out, slamming the door.

"No, you're not," Sniffles says. "You're awesome."

"Come back in an hour," David yells at the door.

"Make that two," Sniffles yells, laughing.

David drops on the bed. "So what are we supposed to do?"

"I want you guys to make love," I say. "I mean, to do what you would do if you were in love with each other."

"With you watching?" he asks incredulously.

"I don't have to be here."

David studies me. "Then what's the point?" Then he gets the point, or seems to, and his eyes jag into Sniffles's, which flare on contact. "Oh, fuck."

"Like you don't know I love you," Sniffles says. His face goes all goofy, like he wants David to think he's half-kidding, or like he's just literalizing my fantasy, but the look comes a little too late and his words sound too rich.

"Shut up," David says. His eyes change, freak, steel.

"No," Sniffles says. "It's the fucking truth. You should be . . . I don't know, proud."

David looks at the floor. "This is the end of our friendship, you know."

"I don't fucking *care*," Sniffles bellows.

David looks up at me, and I look back at him. I mean, for a while. It's intense, but I feel like I owe him. I mean, I guess I am messing things up. Anyway, there's something in his eyes that makes me think he's only just now really thinking about me, like who I am, what I'm doing here. "I fucking hate you," he says, with a slight tremble in his voice. "And you can write that in your bullshit article." Then he stands up and whips, throws, shakes, kicks off his clothes.

"Wait," I say. "I don't want to cause—"

"I need the *money*," David yells.

Sniffles, who's already down to his underwear, walks over to David. He stops about a foot away, hugs himself, lets himself go, shakes out his arms, then lays one of his hands very gently on David's right shoulder. When David doesn't knock it away, Sniffles tips forward and smudges his face on David's neck.

"Oh, fuck," David mumbles.

"Time for me to go," I say. I start for the door.

"Wait," David says. "Stay. It'll help me get into this."

So I pause just long enough to get Sniffles's input, but he's so lost in David. So this is love. On Sniffles's part, I mean. I mean, it must be love. It looks so intense, I can't tell you. "How?"

"I don't know. Just fucking stay, okay?"

"Okay." I look around, then take a seat on this bent folding chair by the window.

David grits his teeth and returns Sniffles's hug. Their hips meet and start to grind. A teardrop leaks out of one of Sniffles's black eyes. David's face is shut tight. It looks like real sex to me.

In my memory of *The Time Machine*, which I haven't watched since late childhood at least, a man invents a contraption that allows him to travel through time. He ends up in a future society where everyone's young, white, blond, spacy, innocent, wearing a toga, and sporting a lame Dutch boy haircut. With the man's help, they overcome some sort of superstitious religious belief they'd adhered to unthinkingly. I think it involves them sacrificing themselves to the gods on their twenty-first birthday or something. To me it was just an amusing, dumb, inadvertently sexy idea. But memory's weird, and maybe the movie's point is that the time traveler's presence or knowledge or values or lack thereof inadvertently ruins something more beautiful than he could ever understand. God, I hope not.

Epistle to Dippy

Pam's fucked. Sue, too, for the moment. They're in a holding cell. Chris, Robert, Tracy, and Goof are abstractions at this point. You can basically forget them. Their bodies are gross to one degree or another. Drew is at Mason's. The latter has come on the former's face several times. Luke's getting stoned with some friends at his soon-to-be former apartment. Scott's at my place. We're sober. It feels kind of nice.

"This needs another level or something." Scott was scrutinizing that daisy-chain drawing. I mean, so intently it mirrored his face. "It's too . . . simple?"

"Acid fallout," I say absentmindedly. I feel like myself for the first time in days. Maybe my life's been improved, I can't tell. "What time's the show tonight?"

Guided by Voices: I can't tell you anything / you don't already know.

"Eight," Scott mumbled. "I don't know about you, but I'm getting right in . . . what's his name, you know, the guitarist's face, and when our eyes meet . . ." He scrutinized his reflection. "Hey, you want a blow job?"

†

I almost forgot we had tickets to Tinselstool. They're an Australian band, very popular at the moment. Stylewise, they belong in the Pearl Jam/Soundgarden/Nirvana camp. Grunge rock, i.e., roughed-up, feedbacky, melodic pop tunes with angry, self-hating, political lyrics. Tinselstool's gimmick is that they're just sixteen years old, and very cute for their age, if you like neo-hippies. Because they're so young, critics have been weirdly kind to the band, finding all kinds of ways to say, "Awww," and all kinds of other ways to avoid saying, "They're too derivative," which is the truth. They're big with the MTV crowd, not to mention with people like Scott and me, who see their music as context, period, a simple, forgettable frame through which to gaze longingly at Daniel James, their angelic guitarist.

"So Luke's moving *in?*" Scott said. He looked shot, tense, unnerved. "I mean . . . are you *sure*, man? I mean what does it *mean?*"

"It means I want him around all the time," I say. I'm skimming a *Vox* article about Tinselstool. It makes them seem goofy.

Guided by Voices: Come on, polluted eyeballs / Stop scouting out the field.

"Yeah, but . . ." Scott cringed. "I mean Luke's cute and everything, but don't you think he's kind of . . . insane?"

Luke's part of a tight clique of friends that predates our first meeting. Most of them live in the small apartment complex in mid-Hollywood where Luke has been crashing for months. First there's Ted, Luke's roommate, an elfin, depressive, extremely tattooed tattoo artist and amateur painter. Carrie's his semi-ex-girlfriend. A fashion designer of avant S&M rubberwear, she's pointedly fierce on the surface, but rather sweet underneath. Richard, a New Wave rock record collector and part-time musician, and his roommate, Frances, a lanky goth stripper, live next door. They've just popped by. So have Andy, a towering, sex-crazed motormouth with a freshly shaved head, and Coffee, a cynical, trust fund–supported late teen with a Hare Krishna coif and a small, cute, extremely pierced face.

"I'm moving in with Dennis," says Luke. He takes a hit off Ted's bong and hands it sideways to Andy.

"Yeah? Well, watch out," Coffee muttered. He frowned, which jiggled the barbells and hoops in his eyebrows, nose, lips, ears.

"Why?" says Luke. "Whoa, this is excellent pot. Uh . . . Oh, right, you mean because of his novels."

Coffee . . . smirks? Hard to tell. "Have you read them? They're all about serial murderers. And all the victims are boys. And all the boys look like you."

They're playing the latest CD by the Black Dog, an English techno outfit that rarely performs live and refuses to be photographed. It's a complicatedly mellow electronic soundscape built around a multiplicitous, danceable beat. Like every CD Luke loves, it has no lyrics, emotions, or intellectual ideas. If you buy into the Black Dog's mystique, their music connects listeners to some sort of ineffable energy source in the collective unconscious or something. It causes one to dance around in a particular way, and the resulting motion effects some temporary biological change whose spiritual benefits outweigh the mere emotional support and/or visceral kick that you get from alternative rock bands like Sebadoh, Guided by Voices, et al. But if you're used to pop structures and vocals and all that, and wary of guru types across the board, the Black Dog just sounds like skillful escapist Muzak with a rather overweening agenda.

†

"So, guys," Ted said. He took a hit off the bong, exhaled, and passed the bong on to Luke. "What's on the social calendar for tonight?"

"*Nothing,*" Luke barks, mock-exasperated. He takes a hit, exhales, and passes the bong on to Carrie. "It's Tuesday. Where do you think we are, Goa?"

The Black Dog: zzkklrfhmmph . . .

Carrie took a hit—or, rather, tried. The pot was ash, so she whipped out her stash. "Well, there's always Potassium," she said, reloading the bong. "I hear it's gotten better."

For all their superficially in-your-face, transgressive-lite, postmodern primitive tastes and attire, Luke's friends are just goodhearted, bright, reasonably creative young nerds. If they hadn't found one another, seen every John Waters film several times, and smoked shitloads of pot, they might be Trekkies, or Internet junkies, or the kinds of guys who skulk around in abandoned factories playing Dungeons and Dragons. Unfortunately for them, their little fantasy trip only seems inordinate when you're inside their clique. From the outside, they look like a thousand other trendily anti-trendy young club kids du jour. Luke joined the clique because part of him loved the offbeat family vibe and because, like the rest of them, some other part of him wants to be cool without seeming too cool. When he's around them he's giddy, superficial, distracted. He's the clique's kooky, lovable mascot.

"I need to use the phone," Luke says. He jumps up and barrels into the kitchen. Dialing my number, he reads the tiny print on a Cheerios box. "Yuck."

"Hello," says my voice. I was expecting . . . I don't know, Chris. He's my most frequent caller. And I guess I'm sort of worried about him and all that.

"It's me," Luke says. Then he waits for the bliss in my voice. There, got it. "Hey, what are you up to? You should come to Potassium. It's supposed to be cool. And . . . *I'll* be there." He knows that's the clincher.

"Uh . . . okay," says my voice. "What time and where?"

Luke's friends are so different from my friends, although a few of our friends overlap, namely Mason and Scott. Still, I think Luke sort of tolerates them out of vague curiosity. Maybe he's flattered by Scott's repressed lust. Maybe he reads Mason's chill as a backhanded compliment. Point is, everyone I care about is either a working professional artist of some sort or significantly younger, fucked up on drugs, and dependent on me for some reason. Everyone Luke knows is artsy, eccentric, adrift. We don't know anyone like each other. I'm hoping that means we're alike in some deep, inexplicable way, i.e., attuned. That our meeting was fated or something. I know that sounds clumsy. If it's not obvious, I'm giving Luke's mystical leaning a shot. I'm thinking of it as some new kind of drug—to begin with, at least. That's my only way in.

"I'm not sure about these." Drew pinched his nostrils. "I keep thinking if they were . . . I don't know, flatter."

Mason squinted. "No, they're lovely." He hunted Drew's face. "My only problem is this." He waggled a finger. "You could lose a quarter inch between your eyebrows and lips."

"Oh, my God," Drew said. He turned away, cringed. "I know, I know. I have a horsey skull. Somebody told me that once."

"It's a minor problem now," Mason said. "But when you're in your twenties, you might look a little sepulchral."

Love's weird, like I said. Maybe it's sort of like those undetectable gas-heater leaks that asphixiate random families in their sleep. It just happens. It's not choosy. It has no discernible logic. It's sort of like death. I mean, in the sense that its travel plans, point, taste, and meaning are too complicated to grasp. Maybe somewhere some anonymous guy did a magic ritual—à la the secretive sort Luke performs—and in the course of bending the universe to his will, the whole world was disturbed very slightly, and one of the shock waves filtered out and aligned Luke and me, or the dwarf and Chris, or Drew and Mason.

"Listen, listen," Mason said. He felt . . . compassionate? That was a first. "Really, Drew, it's not a serious problem. I—"

"No, no, no." Drew was whipping his head side to side, half hoping some sort of centrifugal force would . . . shit . . . he didn't care anymore. "I'm horsey, I'm horsey. You said it yourself."

"Stop it." Mason grabbed for Drew's face. "Remember at Dennis's? All that stuff about cannibalism? Think about it. Would I want to eat you if you weren't amazing?"

I'm never taking acid again. Now I understand what Scott meant. I mean, about acid making art seem pathetic, and how he couldn't think art was pathetic, even if it was. For me, it's more about language. It's fascinating how acid can blur the distinctions between the real world and one's imaginative world, and turn reliable words into free-floating mush. But I'm organized in this particular way for a reason, I guess. Maybe I'm sort of like one of those jailed child molesters who practically beg not to be given parole. They'd rather lie in a cell jerking off with a copy of *Bop* magazine than live a celibate life among evil temptations. It's better for all if I stay locked in here. I.e., friendly and removed on the surface, but secretly lost in impossible thoughts and addicted to putting my weird fantasies into sadly inadequate words.

Backstage at the Whisky, Tinselstool was being quizzed for a *Rolling Stone* feature. "Dude," Daniel said. "Wake up." He chucked a Pepsi at Ben, their drummer. "So what was your question again?"

"Thanks, man." Ben popped the can, glug-glug-glug-glugged.

The journalist was repressing an "Aww." It wasn't easy. "My question was 'Where do you see Tinselstool in ten years?'"

"Oh, wow." Daniel screwed up his face. "I don't know. I guess I see us being really, really popular, and having lots of integrity, and . . . uh, that's a hard one."

When Smear completes its short American tour and flies back to London, Alex will let himself worry re AIDS. He'll do the right thing, wait a few months, and have himself tested—under an assumed name, of course. It'll come back negative. Then he'll be fine, whatever that means. He'll eventually decide that he imagined the whole thing at Mason's. In a sense, the incident will be more of a problem for Damon, who, being Smear's mastermind/songwriter, i.e., its resident artist, and having a clear mental image of Alex, was able to picture his friend being raped, however sketchily, whereas Alex, the perpetrated, was too in denial or something to deal with specifics. So if anyone's damaged, it's Damon. Maybe he'll get a great song out of it. And there's Gargantuan, too, but his mind's too primitive to be read in detail—by yours truly, at least. I imagine he's fine, too, whatever that means.

†

Sniffles is watching TV, so to speak. It's turned on in the room. His eyes are aimed there. They reflect it.

TV: Homer Simpson goes, "Doh!" Bart Simpson makes a sarcastic remark. Marge Simpson goes, "Mmrm." Then Homer Simpson goes, "Doh!"

Sniffles doesn't remember me, David, his family . . . He can't figure out where he's living, exactly. He has no idea why Homer Simpson went, "Doh!"

TV: Lisa Simpson makes a perceptive remark. Maggie Simpson makes a weird little noise. Marge Simpson goes, "Mmrm." Then Homer Simpson goes, "Doh!"

Sniffles raises his hand to his face, scratches. It releases an endorphin or two. When the endorphins kick in, he feels different.

I wrote that *Spin* article over a year ago now. Dora, Warren, and Brett could be anywhere. I'm pretty sure David died quite a while back. At least, that's what I heard. Or should I say that's what Jeffrey Hitchcock supposedly heard through his pedophile grapevine. Word has it that David allowed himself to be kept by some rich older man. Then he got really, really sick. I mean, way too gaunt to turn anyone on anymore and . . . here the story gets blurry . . . he went somewhere else . . . blurriness . . . death. I don't know what to do with that story. It's not exactly fact, and it's not quite a fairy tale, either. Me, I plan to believe what I want to believe. Here's how it starts: Once upon a time, David had a bizarre energy that made excellent copy, and a physical beauty that made one hang on his thoughts, and a violent temper that undercut one's attraction to him, and an AIDS diagnosis that gave his life great symbolism. That's as far as I've gotten.

Sniffles's door opens. He looks there. In walks the clone on his usual rounds. That's familiar. Warmth radiates from that.

"How ya doing, Vincent?" The clone was just thinking out loud, really. He walked to the TV set. "Want this on?"

TV: Bart Simpson makes a sarcastic remark. Marge Simpson goes . . . Click.

"Dennis Cooper asked after you," said the clone. Then he started back toward the door. "Remember him? He said to give you his best."

Sniffles smiles. Nice change. It's not about me. I'm erased. It's just about the rhythm and sound of some meaningless words.

My first love was George. He was a friend's younger brother. I was seventeen, he was thirteen or so. We met at a dance at my high school. I guess he'd tagged along with my friend. George was lost in a bad acid trip, and being sort of an expert on such things, I offered to talk the kid down. I escorted him out to the school's football field, found a deserted spot, and proceeded to mimic Craig's saintly behavior toward me. George was a tall, thin, manic boy with girlish features. He had a terrible sense of the world around him, which I initially read as a sign of his genius, probably because he was cute. We bonded that night, and started hanging around every day after school. He'd drug himself sense-less, and I'd organize our activities. We'd see movies or bands or whatever. He'd act bizarre, and I'd keep him in line. It sounds like hell, and it probably was, but I was completely addicted to him at the time.

Luke's in the backseat with Coffee and Richard. Ted's driv-ing. Carrie and Frances are riding shotgun. They're passing a joint around. That's the Whisky on their left.

"If you haven't heard him, you should," Richard said. He meant Jobriath, this openly gay, early-70's, glam-rock curiosity. "I'll make you a tape."

Radio: kllfmccsxxpp . . .

"I'm getting another tattoo," Carrie said. She leaned close to Frances. "Under my left eyebrow it'll say, 'Super.' And under my right eyebrow it'll say, 'Freak.' Oh, and it'll be written in Arabic. That's the coolest part."

There came this one night. George and I were hanging out at the beach. Laguna, specifically. For whatever reason, George was obsessed with blowing bubbles. He used to get on these jags. He hadn't stopped blowing them all afternoon, usually right in my face. Plus he'd been talking nonstop in this affected French accent he would occasionally adopt. He must have been flying on speed. Anyway, all that nonsense was pissing me off. Like I said before, I wasn't doing drugs in those days, so my tolerance for weirdness was not what it had been—or happens to be at the moment. We were walking along. He blew some bubbles that got in my eyes or whatever. I shoved him, which just revved him up even more. A few minutes later, I lost it. I grabbed him by the hair, hurled him down on the sand, pinned him there, slapped him a few times, grabbed his throat, and screamed, "Shut the fuck up."

Scott pushed through the crowd. It was young, short, and overenergetic. He was old, tall, and senile by comparison. "Sorry, sorry," he mumbled.

I'm content near the back. It's a small enough club. Two guys to my right is the cutest boy I've ever seen in my life. No, wait, he turned his head. Cancel.

"Oh, *God*," squealed some girl to Scott's right. When he looked where she'd looked, Daniel James was strapping on his guitar.

"Hi, everybody," Daniel mumbled into the mike. Aww. "We're Tinselstool, and you guys are really cool for coming out to see us."

†

It was dark by that point. Nobody else was around. We were over by this cliff that had a sea cave carved out in its base. It looked fairy-tale-esque from a distance, but it was really only ten or eleven feet deep and full of trash. That's not the point. Point is, I guess I'd scared George pretty bad, because he shut up for once. I took my hand off his throat. We studied each other. I'd never seen him so calm. I remember deciding I loved him. I had never felt that specific emotion for anyone, parents or otherwise. Not consciously, at least. We both had hard-ons. I was sure that if I leaned down and kissed him, I would have found love. Him too, I guess. I mean in the classical sense, like when you spend your life happily living and sleeping with one other person. But I held back. George was just too insane. I knew that. Our leering contest got awkward. He glanced at his hard-on and laughed uncontrollably. I shrugged at mine. We stood up. I drove him home. Four months later, his dad committed him to a mental institution. He's still there. Once every couple of years I phone the place and ask to speak to George Miles. Then, while the call's being transferred to his room or wherever, I hang up.

Tinselstool: You're gonna die too, bad boy / Bad boy, die till tomorrow.

Scott grinned insanely at Daniel James's ass. The boy was hunched over, playing a solo. He meant every predictable note.

I can't decide. I mean, if I were granted one wish, and the prerequisite was that it had to involve Daniel James, would I ask that he always be happy, or would I ask for a night of wild no-holds-barred sex?

"Dennis!" When I glance to my left, it's this Epic Records geek, Gary something. "I thought I'd see you here," he yelled. "Listen, if you want to meet the band, find me after the set."

†

I've always held myself back. I mean, my whole life. I keep seek-
ing out people like George, hoping the mixture of my fascination
with them and their need for attention will instigate an occasion
through which I could go all the way. I.e., cross-fade myself into
evil, insanity, magic? But when and if the bait does appear, I can't
accept it, I'm not exactly sure why. Instead, I've made myself into
the best friend, caretaker, fuck partner, archivist, and/or beloved
of the beautiful and insane. I know the term "insanity" is vague
and outdated. All I'm trying to say is, I have no idea what I'm after.
I just know how it looks on the surface. Or maybe I can't quite
describe what I'm after, except superficially. Maybe somebody out
there can help me. Maybe Luke will. I wish.

Pam fidgeted in Sue's lap. "So what's our story?" she
mumbled.

Sue was eyeing a swatch of graffiti. It read, EAT ME RAW. "Okay,
listen. This isn't airtight, but . . ."

Sue's plan: Same as before, i.e., they'd parked, made out,
fought. Pam had stormed off, returned. Dead kid? What dead kid?

Pam fidgeted. "Yeah, but . . . okay, you're going to hate me,
but . . . when the cops dust for fingerprints . . . Goof's gonna look
like a leopard. I'm *all over him,* baby."

One last thing. Sometimes I want to see a snuff film so badly it's
painful. It's not that I've gotten too jaded for regular porn. I just
think that if I saw someone kill an attractive young boy, the idea
wouldn't take such a magical turn in my mind. I'd see the gore. I'd
feel the guilt or whatever. I wouldn't see torture and murder as
ways to clean house. I wouldn't want to make cute boys' interior
worlds disappear. I'd know how to perform that particular trick.
That said, I should add that there's this guy I know, Phillip, who

saw a snuff film at a party or something. Or claims he did. Like
me, he'd fantasized about murdering cute boys midsex and all that.
But according to him, watching some elderly guy in a leather hood
kill some cute Mexican teenager just upped the ante. Now Phillip's
even more of a sicko than I am. That's what I'm afraid of. That at
the end of every fantasy, no matter how seemingly concrete, there's
always a "Yeah, but . . ."

Goof was on his way to . . . wherever . . . the morgue? One
paramedic drove. The other paramedic sat in back with the corpse.
That was the procedure.
Radio: Don't leave me high / Don't leave me dry.
Paramedic number two had a bland, mild, midwesternish
look. He was staring at Goof's emptied face. It had this peculiar
pull. Why? Think, think, think.
Goof: kjmmvrhtwqq . . .

Chris is in thousands of pieces that stretch the entire length and
breadth of the dwarf's kitchen floor. It's garbage. The dwarf has
come down from whatever psychotic-esque mood he was in. Reality's
back in position. Chris was just a suicidal, constipated young junkie.
That's all. He knows that now. If he weren't a dwarf, you'd see the
disappointment on his face, or if I didn't see dwarfs as cutesy,
incomprehensible creatures. And another thing. Sue used her post-
arrest phone call to call in a favor from one of her leather-dyke
friends in the S&M community. Said dyke, Kitty Kat, is at Pam's
studio this very minute destroying films, tapes, photos, contracts,
address books . . . So Pam's friends and associates are in the clear.
I mean, as regards the police.

Paramedic number two had a thought. It was ugly. It made
him lift the green plasticky sheet over the corpse's midsection. Just
like a foot.

Radio: What if God was one of us? / Just a slob like one of us?

It was dark under there, but not so black as to disguise this big mole on the corpse's left thigh.

"*Je*-sus." Paramedic number two . . . grinned? That felt weird, but . . .

Eight months ago, paramedic number two, a.k.a. Kevin Lackwell, who's a bit of a sleaze when he's not being paid crappily to act quasi-angelic around sickly people, was allowed to partake in an orgy so-called, orchestrated by one of his friends—make that an acquaintance—whose trip is to re-create scenes from Marquis de Sade novels. In addition to Kevin, his acquaintance, and a few leather daddies, there were two paid attendees—a massively dumb, superhumanly built muscle man and a cute if burnt-out-looking child, almost certainly Goof. They'd reenacted some Oedipal nightmare from Sade's *Juliette*. Problem was, Kevin had always felt guilt afterward re the child. Now, as fortune or misfortune would have it, he didn't have to feel shit anymore.

"Very trippy," yelled Frances. She looked up, down, right, left. Her eyes were all staticked out by Potassium's wicked-cool lighting design.

"Yeah, not bad," Luke yells. He's trying to X-ray the visual clutter. You know, in case Michael's out there being suave, meaningful, misterioso. "Wait. What's this song? I know this song."

DJ: mhklzzxvbbxx . . .

"There," Ted yelled, pointed. He'd just spied a long, empty couch. It was just to the right of the bar, to the left of the booth selling smart drinks.

Mason's chewing Drew's lips. First the top, then the bottom. Not hard, more sort of meditatively. Then Drew sticks out his tongue, and Mason chews that awhile. For his own sake, Drew's struggling not to crack up. As Mason chews, this vaguely salty, saliva-like liquid seeps out of Drew's tissues. Seeing as how he thinks Drew's such a fox, the stuff tastes champagne-like. If Drew weren't his type, it would taste like the stuff in his own mouth, just more gross and extraneous. Eventually, Drew's tongue runs dry, or Mason gets the idea. He leans back, swirls the saliva around in his mouth, and swallows. The taste blends in with the tastes he'd spent the previous ten minutes suckling at length from Drew's ears, eyes, and nose.

"So come *on*," Drew squealed. He slugged Mason's arm. Again. It felt like some major revelation re him was a second away.

"It tastes very fresh," Mason said. "Which makes no sense at all, since you've been eating junk food for, what, fourteen years?"

Drew frowned. "Yeah, but what else?"

"What else? Hm . . ." Mason hocked up some Drew goo, swirled it around, swallowed. "You mean, specifically?"

Drew has a sense, or as much of a sense as you can have at his age, that if he could project himself into the head of someone who's attracted to him, he'd be there. That's how he thinks of it. There, as in happy. He's just smart and/or self-conscious enough to isolate which occasions in life really do it for him. And being cruised by artsy-fartsy older men is number one on his list. As for Mason, he's a lonely older man who makes art because no one is cute and psychotic enough to absorb and require his extreme tastes and interests. But Drew's physical beauty, combined with his love of being flattered, analyzed, and all that, makes him ideal for Mason. So ideal, in fact, that Mason may not even need to make art anymore. Imagine it.

†

I'm watching Tinselstool play their encore. It's bullshit. Point is, it makes the band wildly excited. If you could see them . . .

Tinselstool: There's a kitchen and there is no stove / And the food that it cooks is very hard to love.

Scott had a hard-on. He wasn't proud of the fact, but . . . It wanted Daniel James's rectum around it so badly. I.e., it needed a hug.

"Hey, thanks, you guys," Daniel yelled into his mike. He unstrapped his guitar. "So we'll be back in a few months. See you then."

Tinselstool disappears. Someone turns on the house lights. There's my sweaty friend Scott. We agree that Tinselstool was endearing. The highlight for me was when Daniel James sang the lines "People are killing for no reason at all / It makes no difference if you're short or tall." The highlight for Scott was when Daniel James bent down to retie a shoelace. He'd glanced up at Scott. Scott had yelled, "Hey, you want a blow job?" Daniel James had made a goofy face. What do I think it meant? See, Scott read the goofy element as a maybe. So he's psyched when I find that Gary person. Once we get to the dressing room, Tinselstool's slumped on a couch with two squealing young groupies. Gary announces Scott and me as the band's "oldest living admirers," then turns away and has a businessy word with their manager.

"Hi, how's it going?" Daniel said. His eyes were cold and polite. Then he put his right arm around one of the groupies.

"Oh, fine," I say nervously. "You guys were great. Uh—"

"I'm that guy," Scott interjected. He grinned insanely at Daniel. "You know . . ." Then he mouthed the words, "Hey, you want a blow job?"

"Oh, wow," Daniel said. "Nice to meet you." Then he turned to the girl, whispered something, and they both made goofy faces at Scott.

Pam and Sue have been devising a fairy tale. I.e., an imaginary if somewhat realistic narrative that could supplant their true story. DNA is the problem. Science is so intricate nowadays. Facts aren't just truths anymore. They have molecular structures, subfacts, fractured factual minutiae, et cetera. Goof isn't just some expendable, underage perv, he's the source of a trail of evidence that's a lot more important than his worthless life. He's the biological thing that left traces of meaning on Pam's clothes, in the trunk of Sue's car, across the loading dock, all over Pam's studio. I'm talking data so subtle that no leather dyke in the world could contain it. Point is, Pam and Sue are fucked. No way around it. Reality's just too complex.

Drew was running in place. Mason had clocked him at three minutes, twenty-five seconds and counting. "I'm . . . getting . . . a . . . side ache," he panted.

Mason was watching Drew's ass jerk around. Curious. "I think . . ." He squinted. "Yes, you can stop now."

The second Drew halted, he clutched his right side. "Ouch." The pain bent him in half. Okay, he was being a little dramatic.

Mason had spotted a perfect sweat drop. It leaked from Drew's nape and was still going strong in the small of his back. "Hold still," Mason said. Then he tongued it.

Scott and I are walking back to my car. He can't decide. Should he come to Potassium with me? Or should he phone for a taxi, head home, do some artwork? He's so confused. I mean, about Daniel

James's goofy expression. Did it mean "Stick around"? Or did it mean "You're a fat, ugly, chicken-hawk faggot"? Scott being Scott, i.e., ultra-neurotic, he's tending to favor the latter. Me, I think the kid was naive, showing off for the girl, and at a slight loss for words. Sort of like his music. But nothing's that simple in Scott's universe. Shit, he should have stayed. Shit, he should have kept his fucking mouth shut. Blah, blah, blah. His whining's starting to bug me, so it's not like I care all that much when he ducks into the first empty phone booth.

Luke's staring into the dance floor. It's packed, roiling, liquidy, gleaming. Good old marijuana. "Mmm."

"So you're moving in with Dennis?" Carrie yelled. She hugged Luke. "That's cool. I hear he's into S&M and scat and all kinds of kinky shit. That's cool."

DJ: wmpplsxxkw . . .

"Actually," Luke yells, "I think Dennis is more sort of someone who lives in his head. You know, like me."

Just to reiterate, I'm cool with Luke's feelings toward me, or lack thereof. Here's what I'm thinking: Sex is sort of like being on acid. It's the trip itself that's important. Pills look magical in your hand, but as soon as they're inside your mouth, they dissolve. Then it's up to your mind to make something profound out of their well-disguised chemical compounds. I'm thinking the same thing applies to the people you love. A beautiful, interesting boy can be hot, but his body's the same exact body that's slept with a lot of other people. It's only yours in the process of being absorbed. All of which is to say, the way things have worked themselves out, Luke will always be tantalizingly separate from me. He'll never dissolve into all my imaginative bullshit. Whatever happens to me from now on, good or bad, he'll be safe. That's love, right? Anyway, that's love to me.

†

"So listen," Drew said into Mason's vast ass crack. He was holding his nose, so it wasn't that gross. "If I'd died . . . you know, from that skateboard head thing, what would you have done to me, heh heh?"

Mason thought about that. "The same things I've been doing," he said into Drew's little crack. It tasted gross, but that was sort of the point. "I just wouldn't have anyone to talk to about it."

Drew thought about that. "Do you think I have a weird voice?" he said. "Because sometimes I think it's sort of . . . damn, I always forget that word. Nosy?"

In two weeks and twelve hours, Sniffles will die. The change will be almost too slight to detect—from his viewpoint, at least. Life will be dark gray by that stage, and death will just smudge it a little. That's a guess, need I say. His passing away will be a much bigger deal for the hospice's staff. Since Sniffles's family is untraceable, his remains will be their hot potato. Luckily, there's a standard procedure. One morning the clone will make his rounds, open Sniffles's door, walk in, and the boy will look empty. Then some bureaucratic stuff will occur. Then the hospice will have him cremated. Then one of its lesser employees will drive the ashes out to Pacific Palisades and pour them over a cliff.

I remember this place. It used to be a bathhouse. In fact, right over there, where the DJ booth stands, I fucked a Leonardo DiCaprio look-alike.

DJ: kjjyqwwblppk . . .

I'm rerunning that scene in my head when this cute modern-primitive trendoid walks up. He looks . . . familiar. "Uh, hi," I yell.

"Aren't you Dennis?" Oh, right, it's Luke's friend, what's-his-freaky-name? Coffee. The boy with the shit in his face. "Luke's over there," he yelled.

Did I fuck Leonardo DiCaprio? Is that possible? A friend of mine, Taylor, who claims to be friends with DiCaprio's dad, says the actor is definitely straight. Normally, I wouldn't care. I mean, he's a movie star. He's fodder for dreams, period. It doesn't matter who he fucks in his day-to-day life. But for the sake of this argument . . . It was two years ago, when DiCaprio would have been nineteen. That seems right. The boy was kind of affected. That fits. He wouldn't tell me his name. Check. Based on the nude scenes in *Total Eclipse*, there's a tentative match on the physical front. Point is, if that was Leonardo DiCaprio, I've blown, rimmed, fucked, and shot my come on the face of one of the world's most desirable creatures. If that wasn't him, I had some fun with a beautiful boy who could easily be dead now, for all I know. Okay, it was Leonardo DiCaprio. I think.

Sniffles hears something, looks. It's the door creaking open. Guy enters. Warmth, not exactly sure why. Oh, him. Right.
"It's me," someone whispered. He pulled Sniffles's covers down, rolled the boy onto his stomach, and climbed onto the bed.
When Sniffles is facedown, his ass looks okay. In any other position, it looks like a dinosaur jaw in a bag.
"It's okay," someone whispered. Then he fucked Sniffles hard. No condom, nothing. When he shot up Sniffle's ass, he felt incredibly evil. Nice.

Scott made it home. By then he was extremely depresssed. To make himself feel more depressed, he slumped his shoulders and shuffled around the apartment. Like a sad cartoon character. That made Scott feel more centered. I.e., it put a cutesy aesthetic sheen on his misery. Sort of like his art. Real happiness, in the classical sense, was beyond Scott, except when he had an orgasm, of course. Later for that. He sat down at his worktable, pulled out the "Luke" "comic," read a few frames, realized it was shit, and refiled it. Then he pulled out a blank sheet of paper and did an erotic ink drawing of Daniel James nude. Daniel was hairless and thin, with a gigantic dick and a flat, girlish ass. Then Scott drew a bed around Daniel. Then he drew himself nude, standing next to the bed. He added two voice balloons. In the one by his head he wrote, "Hey, you want a blow job?" And in the one by Daniel's head he wrote, "Shit, yeah. Then I want you to fuck me really hard without a condom."

"Luke," I yell. He's sitting with a few of his trend-enslaved friends. That's a generalization, but it orients me.

"You made it," Luke yells. He stands, hugs me. That feels so sweet, I can't tell you. "I just saw Michael," he adds. "I'm about to go stalk him. Are you okay on your own for a while?"

"Sure." Luke's friends are studying me. Like I said, they're like a trend with a multipart consciousness, so the attention feels goofy. "So which one's Michael?"

When Daniel James scratched his head, the girl licked his left armpit. "Whoa. Ben," he said. "Check this out." Ben was getting a hand job. He checked in with Daniel. "Dude," he said. "Score." They grinned back and forth. Daniel knew armpit-licking was cool if Ben thought it was cool. "That's enough," Daniel said, lowering his arm. The girl switched to his chest. That was cool. Time passed. "This girl's weird," said Ben's voice. Daniel checked in with Ben. Ben was getting a blow job. He looked sort of worried. "She's weird," he repeated, and checked in with Daniel. "Is yours weird too?" Daniel looked at his girl. She was blowing him too. He looked at Ben's girl. She was definitely weird. He looked at his girl again. "Oh, shit," he said. "Ben. Hey." Then he checked in with Ben. "Mine's weird too, dude."

"Dennis," yelled a voice. I'm deep in the club now. When I turn, squint, it's that Coffee kid. "Can I ask you something?"

Coffee had five little barbells through each eyebrow, one through his bottom lip, a heavy hoop hanging out of his nose, and several tinier hoops in each ear.

"You're not going to kill Luke, right?" he yelled. I think he's kidding. "Because some us are concerned." Guess not. Then he turned a crazy ear to my mouth.

"No way," I yell. "Look . . . I'm like you. Only you put scary decorations on your outsides, and I put scary decorations on my insides."

Potassium consists of a bar, an enormous dance floor, a DJ booth, and a stage. Being an indie-rock kind of guy, I've gravitated toward the latter. Occupying the lip of the stage is a long, hyperactive, amateurish chorus line of what appear to be ultra-stoned clubgoers. They've climbed onstage, turned, and faced the crowd, laughing, galloping insanely in place, and pointing excitedly at the people below in perfect counterrhythm to the music. No one's paying the slightest attention to them. It's bizarre. One of them is the star—to my mind, anyway. He's tall and thin, maybe twenty at most, with floppy hair, a boyish face, and extremely loose, wobbling clothes. Unless I'm imagining things, he keeps pointing at me. I mean, over and over and over. Me, me, me. So I point back at him. Him, him, him. After the fifth or sixth mutual jab, he jumps down from the stage, bullies his way through the gyrating crowd, puts his pretty face right in my face, and says, "Hi." He's totally fucked up on Ecstasy. Perfect. I know just what to do with him.

Luke's dancing wildly. It's sort of a ruse. Sure, music's great and all that, but at the moment it's pure camouflage. You know, like the Trojan horse.

DJ: kwllppcbtst . . .

Michael had reddish blond hair, limpid eyes, a wiry torso, pierced ears, and . . . something else. It transmitted a vibe only Luke could receive.

Luke is edging toward Michael. The closer he gets, the weaker he feels. The weaker he feels, the more transparent he grows.

The boy's name is Sun Roof. I've just led him into a stall in the men's room. Sun Roof says he's from Cloud. It's a Radical Faerie commune in San Francisco or something. He thinks UFOs are God's eyeballs. He thinks the diminishing number of UFO sightings means God's losing interest in us. Me: "So there's no reason not to kill people." Sun Roof: "Wow." He can see my point. This is fun. I'm totally into the way his delusions add shading and depth to his beauty. Sometimes I kiss him. He's interested in being kissed. One, it makes his skull feel electric. Two, brotherly love is the UFOs' message. I just slid my hand down the back of his pants. Nice ass. He doesn't care. That's peripheral. I'm not real. I don't even think he can see me that well. I'm the invisible man. He's the ultra-visible man. Something like that. Anyway, we're an interesting couple.

Luke is staring at Michael. Cool, okay. If he concentrates hard enough, Michael will look at him. This is the ultimate test.

Michael was staring at nothing, the op-arty lights, the blurry crowd. Now he turned his head slightly and looked right at Luke.

DJ: vhkpzzwqqbw . . .

Luke's dancing wildly. I mean, for real. The magic stare worked. He can't wait to tell me. Michael isn't the point. He was just like a cross.

Luke is thinking of me. Michael's three feet away, cruising Luke. Across town, Drew's sleeping. Mason is watching him breathe. It's nice. Scott just came. Tinselstool is getting laid. Pam and Sue are in separate rooms being grilled about Goof. Sniffles is sort of unconscious. I'm in a toilet stall kissing that club kid. I'm thinking sex. He's thinking . . . God only knows. It'll all come to nothing, I'm sure. You can basically forget us.